MW01146597

LOVING STRANGERS BY GOD

Short Stories of
Unlikely Encounters
Shaped by the Hand of God

Told by

Archway Publishing books may be ordered through booksellers or by contacting:

Archway Publishing
1663 Liberty Drive
Bloomington, IN 47403
www.archwaypublishing.com
1 (888) 242-5904

ISBN: 978-1-4808-3386-9 (sc)
ISBN: 978-1-4808-3387-6 (hc)
ISBN: 978-1-4808-3388-3 (e)

Library of Congress Control Number: 2016914661

Print information available on the last page.

Archway Publishing rev. date: 09/29/2016

Most adoringly dedicated to my father,

Charles Tabor McLeod III,

a quiet man who never met a stranger.

Save me a seat in heaven!

Contents

Foreword

All happenings, great and small,
are parables whereby God speaks.
The art of life is to get the message.
To see all that is offered us at the windows of the soul,
and to reach out and receive what is offered,
this is the art of living.

Malcolm Muggeridge

Lynn McLeod is alert. She is attentive. She is a noticer. The wonderful stories in this collection come from Lynn's attentiveness to her situation and surroundings, an awareness of what is happening with or to the people around her, and a responsiveness to what is stirring inside her. In an age when people seemingly cannot walk anywhere without earbuds piping in music to drown out dreadful silence, handle the stillness of waiting for their table to be ready, or pause for the traffic light to change without checking their iPhone to find something to alleviate the anguish of being bored or unproductive, Lynn lives with her head up and her eyes and ears open. She suspects God will show up in something or someone, and she doesn't want to miss the experience.

It is said we seek and collect what we highly value. If that is true, then Lynn is a people collector. She does not collect individuals to display them, be seen with them, or use them. She collects people to enjoy them, bless them and learn from them. The great thing about collecting people is you need not guard them or hold them hostage from escaping your life because even the brief encounter becomes an experience and story worthy to keep.

In these stories you'll meet the mysterious and unforgettable Bubblegum Man who blesses children in simple and pure ways, a blind woman and her driver just passing through town, Nekkers and the paperboy, a praying man in an elevator, a physician who makes a surprising choice, and a frightened millionaire.

You'll learn how a woman and her dog brighten the monotonous routine of a morning commute, a homeless man feeds his new friend, and a runner offers clarity in the San Francisco fog.

You'll listen in as two strangers chat in a cemetery, eavesdrop on discomfort and wisdom in a jewelry store, and ponder the housebound conversation between two women of distant ages yet bridged by their hearts.

You'll pull up a nearby office chair and observe the unlikely exchange between a gracious woman and the investigator who intended to ruin her dreams. You'll take a seat in the symphony hall and another by a hospital bed. You'll sit on the steps of a boardwalk and urge a beachcomber to fight a dark undertow.

And as you tour these stories, I hope you are inspired to be more awake and alert to your own stories because new characters, new plots, and new lessons are being sent to you each day. Sent in the form of strangers bearing gifts of love, encouragement, wisdom, and hope. Recognize and welcome them.

Ramon Presson, PhD, LMFT

Acknowledgments

I remain confident of this:
I will see the goodness of the Lord
in the land of the Living.

Psalm 27:13

For me gratitude can only be filtered first through acknowledging the love of my heavenly Father. I am truly inspired by the guidance at the fingertips of His mighty, powerful, and unfathomable hand to write and also granted the courage to press on. Doing so is ultimately how I honor His gift to you, the reader. I am humbled to my very core that God would choose a wretch like me, and along the way offer deeply rewarding joy as I put words on a page. As is His nature, my journey has not taken in solitude for He used many people also worthy of deep thanks.

Ramon Presson, you stood steadfast, coaxing my earliest steps, speaking truth on my good days, and, on the other days teaching me more about myself through the craft of writing. You, sir, are the face of Jesus. Now Lucy can have her darn football! Thank you!

Many strangers in the publishing industry, unbeknownst to them crossed my path, leaving breadcrumbs to follow and producing a powerful impact on this book. Jonathan Merk provided words of wisdom, Dimples Kellogg imparted her honesty, Chip McGregor offered insight into the business of books, Peter Aylsworth delivered his clarity, and William Curry presented the finish line. Thank you!

Countless friends stepped in to walk this journey alongside me. I wish to honor my dear, sweet Linda T., who left the remarkable message on my voice mail days before dancing into eternity. Gary Mc. whose incredible gesture of confidence still leaves me speechless to this very day. Phyllicia S. tended to the steady caring of my soul. Alida O. freely shared her unabashed enthusiasm. Sandra P. C. inspired me with her innocent bravery by claiming victories when it seemed impossible. Nina C. was bold and relentless with her logical direction when it wasn't easy to be. Catherine Mc. spoke delicate, creatively crafted words of loyalty. Barbara W. H. my lovely "sister" who lent final polishing eyes when it counted most. Thank you!

To the unnamed friends, I love you dearly! Your interest, encouragement, and patience with me have been nothing less than phenomenal. And to every single person who may read a hint of his or her story within these pages, yes, you continue to inspire me. Thank you!

Mom, you sacrificed dreams to become a writer into a world of harsh necessity. I share this book to honor what is now our dream. My children, Dylan and Marissa, if there were ever words worthy, I would offer them to you cradled in the love of our heavenly Father. I love you! You are on every page as you are in every moment I breathe. Thank you!

Introduction

There is neither Jew nor Gentile,
neither slave nor free,
nor is there male and female,
for you are all one in Christ Jesus.

Galatians 3:28

Growing up I heard two things: "Don't talk to strangers" and "Stop to smell the flowers." The rebel in me somehow heard a contradiction, triggering a challenge to rewrite both. The first couple chapters in the book of Genesis describe in detail how God first created the beauty on this earth: the light, skies, oceans, land, mountains, and, yes, the flowers. But when He created in His own image, He created man and woman to rule over it, essentially to smell the flowers. Indeed without strangers.

Subsequently the fall of man took place, introducing deceit and leaving fear to begin its treacherous journey within us. On a very real level, it made all of us strangers, oftentimes even to ourselves and ultimately in relationship to God. Deep inside, a miraculous yearning to be known is sewn into the most remarkably intimate places only God knows best. From the first movements within the womb to the last breath we take, "know me" is whispered throughout our lives.

Nothing the world is able to provide will ever answer this. More profoundly, however, is when we see the reflection of our own beauty in the eyes of someone who stopped to smell the flower he or she discovers in us. Not as a stranger but with the heart of God. And from time to time, it is in how we are able to glimpse ourselves beautiful, worthy, and loved. I believe those moments shed a bit of light on God's purpose for the strangers we encounter.

All would be right with the world if we could but only stay locked in such moments of innocence for eternity, surely as it was in the garden.

Yet all is not right with the world. Strangers within us, around us, and left behind in our past all draw us away until, by chance or desire, we stop to smell the flowers. This is where I found the contradiction. What if strangers were actually disguised flowers? What if our reflection witnessed purely, innocently and with the freedom to echo back the honesty of our unhindered beauty could be seen before we murmured, "Know me"? What if secrets within us could only be unlocked through strangers? And what if the beauty in God's creation is especially miraculous when found there?

Make no mistake. There is a serious distinction between strangers and evil. Fear is the camouflage blocking us from recognizing both for what they in fact are, even when the fear is solely based on what a stranger may think of us. Unfortunately I have looked evil in the eye. It was radically different from any experience I've had with someone who I simply did not know.

On the other side of the coin, evil does not restrict itself only to those unfamiliar to us. Tragically it sometimes shows up in the faces of our intimates when we are least frightened. In my mind, putting the tag of fear on a stranger is an avoidable barrier to finding the beauty in some of God's finest and most mysterious art.

We have all been created equal in the eyes of God: young or old, rich or poor, slave or free, male or female, Gentile or Jew, stranger or friend. Once we strip away any impressions coming from sources other than God, we all stand flawed, fearful, and aching to be known. Christ demonstrated how to recognize each other apart from such impressions when He invited a ragtag group of men and women to follow Him, all strangers. I can only imagine how those awkward introductions turned into smelling the flowers, like water into wine.

It has been deeply astonishing to learn truths about myself through an encounter with a person I did not know. When prayers were answered before I mumbled them in uncertainty, or how once I recognized a stranger as a friend, it changed how I could love and be loved by someone in new or unexpected ways even if it happened to be fleeting. For in all those times, I walked away amazed, linking the unpredictable to utter brilliance at the fingertips of the mighty, powerful, and unfathomable hand of God.

As is God's nature, sometimes I have sought out the stranger, and other times I've not. They found me. Even as personally impacting as each encounter has been, I'm convinced the power bound within the encounter reached well beyond me. Nevertheless, quietly and without much falderal, they have brought my life, my journey, and myself closer to God. By talking to strangers, I've come to stop and smell the flowers and to share a foretaste of myself in the garden here on earth.

You will find these pages hold chapters intended as love stories to the very ones who have been such inspirational seeds worthy of growing "Loving Strangers by God." With humility I graciously and undeservingly thank my heavenly Father for inviting me to join Him in loving them all.

Chapter 1: The Gentleman

Be still and know I am God.

Psalm 46:10

Beyond the row of four-story brownstones and just to the left of the stoplight, two hundred and seventy-eight steps led to an interruption from the towering city, exposing an enchanted pathway. Through it, an aged and winding cobblestone corridor divided two rows of flowering cherry trees. Each with limbs twisting in contrast to its gentleness, holding close delicate petals of the palest pink, designed specifically to tempt a slight shadow into igniting as it cast between each flowering clump. The fragrance of the branches swayed with the breeze, tenderly welcoming one's senses to follow. If the glossiness of the sky had been any bluer, it would have been a different color. And yet she hardly noticed.

The pathway was a shortcut taken for granted as her natural rhythm matched that of the city - hurried, hectic, and unyielding. Each time the sole of her shoe snapped with the harshness of the cobblestone, her pace was defined even as her purpose wasn't. There was no time calling for either an arrival or a destination. Even so, she trudged on as if it took precedence over everything else for the day. And with it came quietly denied whispers from the lonely places of interrupted sleep from the night before when she yearned for a glimpse of something beautiful. In daylight it would evade this very moment.

Strangely and without noticing, not a single person traveled the corridor either with or against her. As she rounded a bend, the path led to a fork, prompting a verdict to either loop back or continue toward the arrival waiting on the other side of the city. She paused. In the distance a gentleman rested on a shiny, coal black bench nestled between rows of matching street lamps. Planted in between each, the purple creeping phlox had grown only slightly taller than the squirrel scampering about in a flurry to discover its own folly.

The gentleman's hair was salt and pepper gray, cut short with scattered curls just above the collar of his light blue shirt then randomly twisting about his forehead and above each ear. He wore a khaki jacket with trousers that nearly matched in color. Neither showed a single wrinkle as his posture mimicked the torso of a perfectly posed mannequin. The hands, now resting in his lap, were kind. Yet in searching his face, she was captivated by the seemingly flawless combination of ruggedness and the gentleness of purity.

In her hesitation to evaluate choosing the loop or not, the gentleman nodded in her direction with an invitation to follow the pathway leading toward him. The snapping of her shoes became muffled as her pace relaxed into an unanticipated sigh, seemingly left over from exasperation. Despite a softening in her stride, her awareness continued toiling in a far too familiar game of hopscotch played with the pointless, contemptible thoughts for matters long gone. Uneasiness swirled as recognition of the void between the gentleman and her. She did not consider any of it as she drew closer. Instead she lingered on her side of the tension just long enough to misunderstand how truly drawn she was to him.

As providence would have it, the squirrel scampered up to the place only inches beyond her foot. It paused, resting back on its hind legs, looking up at her curiously and then back over its shoulder at the gentleman now only a few yards away. From the soulful black eyes of this furry, little scamp, she was tenderly guided to the eyes of the gentleman resting on the bench. They were unlike any she had ever seen before, deep and full of indefinable colors with light radiating from within him.

She was flattered to have him looking at her. Perhaps she glanced down, blinking her eyes and blushing, but she couldn't be sure. It felt as if she had. Initially the gentleman's watching was a curiosity. Who was he, and why was he? Ever so subtly, the questions turned inward searching. Why her? What about her drew his attention? A hyper alertness to her otherwise unconscious actions triggered nervousness, to the very point of negotiating with herself. Should she brush the hair on the right side of her face aside or not? Was the posture of her stride prim and proper, as her grandmother had taught? And would the prickling on the back of her neck disappear without being scratched? Every step funneled into a forced deliberation as the flattery slipped away, replaced by apprehension.

In approaching the gentleman, she said nothing. They shared no gesture or polite exchange. He simply watched, unwavering. The time for a courteous introduction passed away, leaving the distance between them to age. His attention took on a sensation of eeriness masking her otherwise disciplined alarm to flee. Yet she persisted in her negotiations, no longer for appearance sake but in search of solace. It didn't come.

Instead she gathered the courage to gaze back, eye-to-eye with the same deliberation and eager to have her apprehension become his. The insidiously slow motion and subtlety of his smile stated with certainty the mercy he caressed in her distress. He was quite solemn.

She closed her eyes, pretending he had vanished. She freely flipped her hair to the side, slouched her shoulders forward into rebellious relief, and soothed the small hairs standing erect on the back of her neck. She waited listening and heard nothing until the very exact moment when at last she opened her eyes. Planted within her, a seed of restlessness yearned to comprehend why he watched or what he saw. And most carefully, why her?

The gentleman stretched out his hand, tenderly speaking simple words touching in the quietest places, protected from the world she knew, "I've been waiting for you. Please join me."

Taking the final steps toward the bench, she accepted the invitation to sit next to him. His eyes pursued hers in a deliberate gesture of protection as she positioned herself on the bench a few inches to the right of where he waited. She was finally safe. He tenderly took both her hands in his, and she gazed down to study the two pairs now resting in her lap. Yes, his were kind even as they echoed a mighty, powerful, and unfathomable nature. Held within them was a mystery she did not understand but knew to trust. She could not look beyond their fingers laced together in solitude. In them stillness grew.

Quietude began to invade the hurriedness as the moments served to compliment her introduction to a fresh sense of wisdom. Time vanished in their silence and, with it, the surrounding life of the city. She was still. Intertwined in his single gift were love, joy, peace, patience, kindness, goodness, faithfulness, gentleness, and self-control. Aaaahh, if she could but only be held in this gentleman's hands for eternity.

"You will only find yourself in the beauty of my creation," he softly whispered.

Looking up from their hands, she saw the sun and how brilliantly it imparted warming affection from beyond the treetops until it coddled the cheeks of her face. In a gracefully lingering dance, the clouds highlighted how crystal bluely the sky caressed the tips of the pink cherry blossoms. Below, twisting branches from the sturdy trunks of the trees reached to encourage, nourish, and provide for each fragile blossom. Leisurely dropping from within the midst of the pink, a petal floated ever so elusively until it faithfully settled on the cobblestone walkway. Solid as time, the well-worn cracks of the stones secretly told the story in the lives of bygone travelers. Trickling from the corner of her eye, a tear fashioned a path just as the petal had. Here the mystery of her lay throughout eternity within the beauty of his creation.

Searching eagerly to grasp for the significance of it all, she returned back to the eyes of the gentleman, only to find he had moved from being by her side to being in her heart.

Chapter 2: The Bubblegum Man

He will cover you with his feathers,
and under his wings
you will find refuge;
his faithfulness will be your
shield and rampart.

Psalm 91:4

The whistle of the Bubblegum Man had been around as long as she could remember and before perhaps. There was no certainty when she first knew he would round the corner with gaiety to share along with the pink, sweet treats hidden in his pocket. He simply was. At the age of six or seven, one assumes everything is just there, hardly with questions or a savvy spirit for discerning. In her mind, the bigness of grown-ups was mirrored in his rounded belly and head without hair or camouflage. Much like his shabby clothing, his pie-shaped face was well worn, protecting a surprise peeking from his eyes. Squinting through cheeks colored by a grin of mismatched teeth was the spry and jolly invitation.

It was the early 1960s, before race riots, sex, drugs, and rock 'n roll or when a neighbor was first a suspicion to be vetted by formal introduction. As the legend goes, children did play outside in the dirt until the streetlights came on or they heard someone's mother three blocks over yelling an exaggerated name in warning to the world. She was on their trail, and it was time for them to hide. Poverty wasn't masked with cheap toys, for they instead had each other to chase with sticks found under the bushes. Games were limited only by imagination, energy, and the camaraderie of those running rowdy in the neighborhood. Fences were nowhere to be found. The shortcut between one place and another was often down a gravel alley or across the backyard of old ladies who hosed down their driveway every Monday, Wednesday, and Friday morning before nine a.m.

For neighborhood children, limits were set by the number of blocks they were allowed to travel in any one direction before asking permission from an adult or parent to venture beyond. The answer was generally a resounding no. Railroad tracks with trains screaming in the distance described a world worthy of ignoring, nevertheless persistent in swirling outside their own. Any random front porch railing was purposed for practicing high-wire routines with fledgling hands reaching out for balance to corroborate courage. Erratic ruptures in sidewalks formed the challenge for a game of hopscotch, and the curbs of the streets were benches to take a load off.

The rules and discipline were far more unspoken than written. And remarkably the children all knew how to play together without them. Skinned-up knees and elbows were part of bouncing back. Pebbles ground into a scrape were something they shook off to consider another day. From time to time a squabble would break out between a couple of the older kids, prompting everyone to chase them into the secret fighting place to gather around, waiting intently for fisticuffs to solve the dispute or make a liar of the other. In all of it, not a hand was raised, and quarrels were resolved when one or both kicked the ground with a declaration of "I double dog dare ya!"

The place they called a park was a run-down neighborhood schoolyard surrounded by cement and where two picnic tables sat on either side of the tetherball pole. It was a gathering spot destined to cook up the adventures of the day from their own creativity. Once a month the rotating park leader would teach them how to weave three cents of thin, plastic strips they called bondoogle into key chains and necklaces. Girls learned how to fold notes into contortions to hide secret crushes and grudges. Combed hair, clean or matching clothing, were all left for mothers to fret about on special occasions. Lightning bugs, frogs, and worms were captured in jars or slipped into pockets for safekeeping. Dandelions were respected as real flowers picked intentionally to impress as a small gesture of affection or soften the heartstrings of a parent who came calling with a punishment to dole out.

The days were just long enough. And the summers never were. Such is how they passed one day after another without counting. During such tender years, time is random, and so was the magic of the Bubblegum Man's whistle. It conjured a formidable announcement to indeed chase after the sweet, soft, pink treats. He had no name or calling card. She wondered if he intentionally stood barely out of sight and just around the corner from where he heard them playing. It served as the perfect vantage point to watch the jumping, running pack of greedy little munchkins clamor for first place and squealing, "It's the Bubblegum Man! It's the Bubblegum Man!"

Holding the coveted piece above their heads, they jumped to grab at it as he waggled the first wrapped treat just out of reach. At the precise point when their enthusiasm would have converted to frustration, the Bubblegum Man released it into the grubby hands of one of the taller kids. Off they scampered, leaving the rest to wait patiently as the Bubblegum Man reached into his pocket one time for each child.

Bestowing a gesture of distinction in every piece, he would say, "Awww yes, this is the one I brought just for you."

She was not sure if it were her size or wonderment, but he always seemed to reserve the last one for her with an underlying designation of extra special. She was accustomed to lingering behind as the pink bubblegum-puffing rascals all jaunted off to battle over who could blow the biggest, perfectly round, or loudest-popping bubble. For her the challenges were well beyond her aspirations, and besides she was intrigued to learn what might be left in his pocket. Ever protective of his secrets, the Bubblegum Man swatted away her hand as she tried to reach in for one more piece to save for later.

To an outsider, the two must have looked quite the pair walking down the block, swinging their arms in practiced unison. With him, big, round, and boastfully taking his next step, she scampered to keep up in hopes of drawing a reaction suitable to earn another piece of bubblegum. Every once in awhile he would chuckle over something she hardly thought funny. In response she purposefully scrunched her face, showing displeasure for how easily he found humor in the seriousness of their bubblegum courtship.

Once they reached the end of the block, inevitably he patted her on the head, saying he would see her again sometime and she was to be good and obey her parents. His swagger as he rounded the corner was that of a prideful man imitating Santa Claus when he mounted a rooftop sleigh after secretly leaving Christmas cheer below.

The Bubblegum Man mysteriously walked in and out of their summers until she became old enough for an introduction to the injustices of this world and moments before bubblegum lost its attraction. Remembering when she heard his whistle for the last time was far more distinctive than when she heard it for the first time. Running to greet him just as she'd always done, she noticed a police squad car pull slowly past her, stopping by the curb where he stood.

Facing the opposite direction of traffic, two officers got out of the car with one hanging back by the rear bumper and the other approaching the Bubblegum Man with his hand on his holster. She wasn't near enough to hear what they said to each other but watched carefully from behind a flowering shrub she used as a hideout. The pink petals and soft smell made her feel like a safe little spy.

The Bubblegum Man shook his head, taking the soft, sweet treats from his pockets to show the police officer. The bubblegum was then taken from him and handed back to the officer's partner standing by the rear of the squad car. After being asked more questions, the Bubblegum Man shrugged his shoulders, turned around, and put his arms behind his back for the police officer to put on handcuffs, guide him to the backseat of the car, and shut the door.

It was the first time she had seen a police car actually stop, let alone witness officers question someone. She was afraid to come out from behind the bushes, believing she too would be handcuffed. In a child's mind, unimagined dots are connected quickly, and for her, she was convinced she could certainly go to jail for accepting bubblegum from him. The other kids had run away, gone home, and were busy describing the happenings to their mothers. Yet she was certain their escape was protection from also being arrested.

Mixing confusion with her fear, she rationalized going to jail for bubblegum or any of the multitude of things she didn't know would get her in trouble. The Bubblegum Man had told her to obey her parents, but they had not warned her not to take a treat from him. She waited endlessly for the squad car to pull away, providing a safe escape to run home and tell her dad before promising to never do it again. As she waited, she practiced her plea in her head. But the police car didn't move and didn't move and didn't move.

Finally the front passenger side door opened. Stepping out, the police officer that had previously lingered at the back of the car opened the rear door for the Bubblegum Man. Once he stepped out, the officer unlocked his handcuffs, gave him a strict nod of the head, and began talking sternly. The Bubblegum Man nodded in response just as one of the other kid's mothers came running up to the scene by way of the closest alleyway. The angry mother approached the officer pointing, shaking her head, and looking as if she were scolding the policeman.

From behind the bushes, she was frightened for the woman because it seemed to her that going to jail was easier than she thought. All the while, the Bubblegum Man stood absolutely stiff, no longer nodding his head but instead hanging it down as low as it could go. The robust nature she had come to know him by had vanished. The police officer handed him back the bubblegum and then left.

The angry mother flung her arms around the neck of the Bubblegum Man, hugging him. A moment later he stepped back from her reassurances, turned, and walked home. Once the mother retreated in the direction from where she had come and after waiting for the coast to be cleared, she followed the Bubblegum Man to a two-story white building with five mailboxes posted on the front stoop.

Looking over her shoulder, she could see it was an entire block beyond the border of where she was allowed to travel without permission. She watched him take each step up to the front door, pull out a key, unlock it, and go inside. He looked like a beaten old man.

Later that evening when her father arrived home from work, she asked him, "How could someone go to jail for bubblegum?"

He simply told her, "Don't talk to strangers." Saying nothing more.

The next day she couldn't shake the feeling something was wrong and she needed to fix it. She went back to her dad for more answers.

He asked her, "Do you know the man's name?"

"Of course I do! He is the Bubblegum Man!" she snorted with confidence.

Her father thought he put the matter to rest by saying, "You need to be careful. A stranger could be dangerous."

She didn't believe his message. How could bubblegum be dangerous? The whole thing confused her even more with no answers, no explanation, and no reasons. And the Bubblegum Man had changed. It wasn't the treat she was concerned about losing; instead it was her friend.

A few days later, she snuck over to the house she had seen him go into. When she tried the door, it was locked so she waited on the front step until a raggedy old woman carrying a bag of groceries approached.

"Does the Bubblegum Man live here?" she asked.

The raggedy old woman laughed before opening the door. "I suppose he does. On the second floor, third door on the right. Here, I'll let you in if you help me carry the milk." She handed her the carton to lug inside and to the first closed door on the left.

The house smelled like boiled potatoes and was dark with creaky sounds each time one of them took a step. The light bulb in the ceiling didn't have a cover, and the windows on either side of the door were blacked out. In the background she could hear the noise from at least two or three televisions tuned to the same channel. Up the steep stairway, she counted twenty-one steps. Although she couldn't see well enough to know for sure, she suspected it was dirty in a shabby run-down way as a consequence of many years of neglect.

Although the house was much like other surroundings she knew well, it gave her the same queasy feeling in her stomach that something was wrong. Upon getting to the top, she counted three doors on the right and knocked.

She wasn't sure what she wanted to say to him until the door opened.

"Hi! I need to find out if you are a stranger or not," she blurted out.

His familiar laugh accompanied a gesture to enter the apartment. "Come on in, sweetie," he said.

The tiny room was clean and neat with light streaming through the open windows. On one side, a twin-sized bed was made up with a light blue cover. A small, kitchen table was next to an open sink with a miniature refrigerator situated in the adjacent space. The stove just to the right was littler than any she had seen before. In the middle of the room was a round, braided rug. And by the windows a gray, overstuffed chair with a matching ottoman faced a tiny television resting on an end table. Underneath it was a radio playing piano music, soothing and quiet with pretty melodies.

Resting on the arm of the chair lay open a brown, leather-bound Bible with gold letters. It was the finest item in the entire room apart from the sunshine streaming in over the top of it.

"Would you care for a drink of Coke-a-cola?" he asked.

"Sure," she answered, soaking in every detail of his room.

It was contradictory to the rest of the building. It suited him. Bringing a small bottle from the refrigerator, he poured a quarter of it into a little clear glass, added an ice cube from a bowl in the freezer, and handed it to her as he patted the ottoman for her to sit.

"So tell me. What is going on in that little head of yours?" he asked.

"I thought you were going to jail for bubblegum," she answered through the swig of the cola. The fizz tickled her nose. It tasted sweet.

"No, honey, the police officer just had a couple questions for me. It is all right now. So don't worry, okay?"

"Will you still be the Bubblegum Man?"

"Honey, I'll always be the Bubblegum Man, even if I can't give some to you kids any more. Sometimes it is better to help others feel safe when they are fearful. Nothing anyone thinks of you can ever be made true simply by what they say. Truth is truth, regardless of what someone thinks of it. Do you understand?"

"I'm trying to, but it isn't fair." Her heart was beginning to feel sad for both of them.

"Look outside. What color do you think the sky is?"

"Blue," she answered.

"Okay, if I said the sky were orange, would it change colors?"

"No."

"That is because the truth is . . ." he paused. "It is blue. And regardless of what anyone says, it is still blue. That's what I mean, honey. Just because someone may have been frightened because I gave you bubblegum, doesn't make it scary. I think it is best for all of us if I try real hard not to frighten them anymore. What do you think?"

"I think they don't know you. If they did, they wouldn't be scared. I'm not."

"Sometimes it is exactly that easy, and other times it's not. What I want you to remember is truth is not scary and cannot be changed even when someone is scared of it."

An upbeat and jovial song played on the radio, mimicking how the Bubblegum Man had been before.

She asked, "Can you turn it up a little so I can hear it better?"

He did. Something about the sunshine, truth, and music inspired her to dance. She twirled around in the middle of the braided rug with her arms swaying to the tune as she shuffled her feet and flung her long hair this way and that way about the room. The Bubblegum Man clapped his hands and tapped his foot to the beat. She felt beautiful, safe, and loved.

When the song finished, he placed the empty glass in the sink and guided her to the door.

"You are a wonderful dancer. No one is better. I have some chores to do now, so I'm going to have to say good-bye."

"Do you have a name?" she asked, wanting to tell her dad once and for all that he wasn't a stranger.

"Why sure. It is the Bubblegum Man. Now you scoot along, honey. And don't forget what I told you. Be good and obey your parents."

"I will. I promise," she replied.

He walked her down the stairway and out the front door. About three quarters of the way down the block, she was close to crossing back within the boundary where she had permission to go. Turning back, she saw he was still standing in the doorway. Waving, he motioned for her to go on as if he were waiting for her to reach safety before he would turn to shut the door between them.

At that precise moment, she recognized the mighty, powerful, and unfathomable hand of God's protection. On the sidewalk in front of her lay a small, white feather. Stooping down to pick it up, she began to run home with outreached arms mimicking how she imagined the feather to be vast wings clearing a path for truth to guide her. Truth would always remain her refuge.

Chapter 3: The Blind Author

And those he predestined, he also called;
those he called, he also justified;
those he justified, he also glorified.

Romans 8:30

There was nowhere in the mirror to escape the fear. It was enormous and growing far more rapidly than the deadliest virus. Truly witnessing the extent of how it performed on her face revealed another side she wasn't prepared to see. Still there it was in her eyes, the color of her skin, the wrinkles of her brows, and even the way her nostrils flared. Earlier tears now marked her cheeks with subtle tracks of dread. She was leaving home.

It was not her nature to cry easily. She was always the one to protect vulnerabilities with an unmatched privacy. Seeing them in the mirror alarmed her. How could so much be revealed in a momentary glimpse as she passed from her bedroom to the bathroom in search of a box of tissues? The glimpse forced her to stop, look, and ultimately know what the fear intended to show. It was the defining moment when she recognized there was no going back. To the world this was a normal Tuesday morning.

"Oh, dear Lord, please help me to know the next step is Yours."

The safest direction was in prayer to her Savior. Any other way would simply feed the paralysis of fright. Turning from the image in the mirror, she dropped her head and watched the lingering tears land on the marble bathroom counter as she whispered for help. She could not bear to look again. Similar to a wave of comfort one feels from being wrapped in the folds of a bold hug, her screaming thoughts began to relax.

She heard it, a message from the Holy Spirit, so often coming as prayers are spoken. "Go to Suzie Tuesday's."

In many respects it was odd yet unmistakably clear. Joining a Bible study her pastor's mother, Suzie, gave on the last Tuesday of each month wasn't exactly what she anticipated. However neither was the fear. Given a choice between each, the preference was fairly evident. She could grab the box of tissues and return to bed where the false reassurance of solitude would hide the ugliness. Or she could merely turn the knob of the shower toward hot and take the first step away from the mirror.

Make no mistake. The familiar ritual of showering and dressing could not be taken for granted this day. It wasn't simply an exercise in primping. Instead it was a reluctant act of obedience. There was nothing in her - specifically in her plans or her nature - that would risk publicly exposing her vulnerability, particularly when she felt so fragile. Her solitude had been well rehearsed. Fear had not suddenly reared its ugly head in one fell swoop or one unsuspecting day. It had very insidiously plucked its way into her psyche one tiny experience at a time. Risking its exposure, in fact, fueled the fear, giving air for it to breathe.

Leaving the familiar shelter of her hometown, were radical steps she didn't expect to stumble through, if not clumsily fall upon. The closing on the sale of her house was scheduled in a few days. The movers would begin packing the truck. She would move to Tennessee and attend seminary at a small private university. She didn't know anyone living there and barely knew the directions needed to arrive. The decision had been abrupt.

It had only been a few short months since accepting Christ as her Savior. After living a lifetime on the other side of the veil, she encountered Damascus, much as Paul had. Similarly she experienced a hunger to follow an unprecedented journey marked by learning and sharing the Gospel. For today, in the mirror and in her fear, she hadn't discovered Paul's story yet.

Coming from a background where she wasn't aware there was an Old or New Testament meant an avalanche of learning followed. Broad gaps remained scattered about in her knowledge of the Bible. Only by the unmatched hand of God, her desire, opportunity, and resources aligned perfectly to enable a remarkable indulgence to pursue them. It did not come protected from interference of the world, evil, or even her. Fear is insidious, and she was learning for the first time the depth of power it could hold.

However, its power was a mirage in the stillness of His Word. Romans 8:15 says, "*The Spirit you received does not make you slaves, so that you live in fear again; rather, the Spirit you received brought about your adoption to sonship. And by him we cry, Abba, Father.*" God loves His babies.

With outstretched arms coaxing her to release her grip on safety, His voice was clear. "Take one step."

She turned the knob of the shower.

The Bible study was held once a month in the private room of a restaurant. She was familiar with the class only to the degree of having attended a couple times.

After walking into the room, she searched for a seat, hoping to find a place beside someone she knew. The room bustled with far more activity and far fewer recognizable faces than she expected. No one knew her name. She walked past a barrage of small tables embellished with purses used to reserve someone's spot, trays displaying an assortment of food, and women cheerfully chatting. There was no place for her. Any confidence she would stay began to rush out the door in the same direction she was soon to follow.

Turning to escape, she spotted the red triangle with the number seven held in her right hand. It was intended to direct the waitress to deliver food she'd ordered and paid for, to the table she didn't have. Tingling rose in the back of her already swollen eyes. Her legs felt weak, and by this point, she had used her failing energy to get this far. She was exhausted. It was the type of weariness unique to emotional grappling a moment before surrender. She dropped her head down to her chest in an effort to disguise any vulnerability. Reaching to steady herself, she found the back of a chair parked too close to notice in her line of sight. Next to it was a table with three seats and two Bibles. It was easier to sit than to leave.

The two women who joined the table were not typical suburban Christian women on a Tuesday morning outing. A late fiftyish blonde woman sans makeup with a stocky build in frumpy attire jostled for the seat by the wall. Her left arm extended out in the shape of an L with a bulky white cast supported by two protruding rods connected to her side. The other woman chose the seat with her back to the crowd. She was tiny, fragile, and elderly. Much older than her companion. She too was dressed in leftover and ill-fitting clothing. In contrast to her partner, she had dark brown skin and was blind.

"Okay, God, I get it. You have me at the broken kids' table." She thought to herself.

Once they settled in, she asked the women with her arm in the cast, "Do you have a broken wing?"

"No," she said, "I'm battling cancer and have had all my lymph nodes removed."

The woman's answer alone was enough motivation for her to shrink back and put her head down in an effort to concentrate on eating. It was rude perhaps and, in many respects, out of character for her. Nonetheless engaging in the details of someone else's struggle was more than she was equipped to manage. She didn't share a word, make eye contact, or acknowledge they were at the table. She simply tried to dissolve into the self-protective shield of anonymity.

She was learning such a place of discomfort laced with vulnerability is fertile ground for God to gently speak. Suzie's lesson taught her for the first time the story of Paul's conversion. In her description of Acts 9, she heard how dramatically God uses the very things she harbored in herself as flaws and inadequacies. Both Paul and she were well educated, professionally successful, and blind until God revealed Himself. Neither fit the presumed mold, and both yearned at all costs to chase the calling God put on their lives.

Suddenly much of the isolation she felt was lifted. But it wasn't because she believed she was like Paul, for in their comparable stories also lie vast differences. More aptly it displayed the mighty, powerful, and unfathomable hand of God in everyone's life.

Suzie also continued by teaching tools to discern God's plan. She essentially advised, if someone hesitated or questioned a situation, he or she should try pulling out of it. If it were truly God's plan, He would pull them back into it. And if it weren't they would discover He didn't. The decision she made to leave home carried many, many, many layers apart from God were unexplainable. Within her a desire, vaster than any love she knew, fervently sought to learn everything she missed about her Father while living on the other side of the veil.

Suzie's words landed precisely where God intended for her to receive them, in a place where tears of fear could be brewed into tears of joy. She recalled specifics from the first whispers she heard from God and how they tumbled out in an arbitrary search on the Internet about seminaries. How she listened to an online sermon hours later.

Then the next day she heard the same message preached at church and then finally later in the evening from a girlfriend at a Bible study. It was clear. She was to apply for seminary. The obstacles of time, resources and opportunity vanished.

With only forty-eight hours looming to meet the required application deadline for acceptance into the program, she obeyed. The college transcripts from twenty years earlier, character references, the thesis paper about her testimony, letters of recommendation, and entrance interviews had all been accomplished. She was accepted.

Immediately the obstacles hit hard with a storm causing roof damage on her home; a few days later her finished basement flooded. Both were repaired before selling her house within a week for 100 percent of the asking price. Very serendipitously she found a home to lease when she moved. The details had been a whirlwind of stop and goes. They were not little details, but instead it was world versus God details. It was no wonder she was exhausted with an overdose of fear.

The woman with her arm in the cast leaned closer, "Sweetie, I saw your tears. If there is something heavy on your heart, I would be happy to help you carry it."

The thought struck her as odd since the woman wasn't able to carry her own hamburger to the table.

"Suzie's lesson was just what I needed to hear today. Thank you," she softly answered.

The enormity of her realization that God confirmed she was to be moving without fear felt suggestive of a dam breaking if she dared venture into sharing a single detail.

"Me too," she said. "I've just figured out the direction I thought I was to go isn't what God wants for me because I'm putting myself in against God pulling me out."

"Aahh yes, I can see that," she said, "but my tears were from joy as God has confirmed for me that I'm headed in the right direction."

Her answer prompted the blind woman to intentionally take her hand, asking with the tenderness of humility, "My sweet girl, if I might ask, what is God calling you to do?"

"I'm moving to Tennessee to attend seminary," she blurted with little regard for buffering in niceties or manners.

"Yes, now I understand why we are here today."

And with a kind nature, the blind woman told a story of her journey from New Jersey to Texas to attend seminary at the age of sixty-one. The story spoke of the obstacles not only of getting there but also how because of blindness, the textbooks were not readily available. Making friends or finding a church didn't come any easier. In all of it was the advantage of seeing God even though she couldn't see the world.

Generating an unheard anthem to God's glory, she began stumbling all over herself with "Oh my words" and "Oh my gosh" for the vividness of the blind woman's testimony overshadowed her diminishing fear. The story didn't end there. Finishing seminary wasn't the stepping-stone toward working in ministry as the woman hoped. Her blindness remained an obstacle leaving her to cry out for God's purpose.

The Holy Spirit laid it on her heart to write an inspirational book of poems based on scripture. The blind woman explained in morning prayers God had given her two poems to share that very day. She invited her to choose either "Lord and Master" or "I'll Lift You Up Again." The latter was chosen.

Leaning in as one would for a private prayer, the blind woman whispered the poem into her ear. *"Child, don't you worry. I know the plans. I'll lift you up. I'll lift you up again. Take your mind off the problems. Keep your focus on me. I'm the one who will solve them. Just wait, be still, be still and let me."* Once the prayer was finished, she kissed the beautiful, frail woman on the cheek, knowing one of God's army angels was purposefully sitting at the broken kids' table specifically for her. Rarely do we find ourselves in one of those moments we want to last an eternity but understand it won't.

Hoping to find another time when they would cross paths, she asked the blind woman, "How long have you been going to this church?"

"No, no, sweetie. We are not from here. We are traveling from Texas to Chicago for my book signings. We stopped to get a bite to eat and saw the sign on the door for the Bible study. Suzie was so kind to let us join you."

The woman with the cast was the driver. They would be leaving in a few minutes.

Fear is an insidious demon unmatched by the mighty, powerful, and unfathomable hand of God.

James,

I truly pray you find a treasure or two in these stories.

Be well and enjoy!

Lyn

Chapter 4: The Retired Muckraker

Whatever you do,
work at it with all your heart,
as working for the Lord,
not for human masters,
since you know that you will receive
an inheritance from the Lord as a reward.
It is the Lord Christ you are serving.

Colossians 3:23-24

The bundle came just as it always did, with thin, white plastic twine securely tied around a stack of newspapers, basket-woven in groups of ten. The 5:20 a.m. thud on the front porch seemed to be more reliable than even the alarm clock his grandmother had given him for his twelfth birthday.

"There is no need for a paper route if you aren't going to be dependable," she challenged him.

Somewhere between the thud and watching her drink the first cup of coffee while she read the local news, he felt the scrutiny of what she meant. It was easy to snap the rope with the pocketknife his grandfather bestowed on him with an equal warning of responsibility. Missing both points completely, he dreaded the tedious sorting, rolling, rubber banding, and loading his gray canvas bag with the large red newspaper logo written across the front. Learning about dependability or responsibility wasn't quite what he had in mind. Piquing his interest was actually the twenty-one dollars a week plus tips promised by the route manager. If he saved up, he could be a millionaire someday or buy the red Schwinn bicycle on page 392 in the Sears and Roebuck catalog. At the moment, both seemed outlandish as he returned the knife to his back pocket and began.

Through the sorting, he wondered if the inspiration for their lectures on being twelve were linked in some way to the perks of being grandparents of the paperboy.

"There was something to this," he thought.

They didn't have to open the front door, walk the three steps to the edge of the green-painted porch, and wonder if the news had been delivered properly or not. It was simply waiting on the kitchen table when they came down for breakfast. From time to time he would see his father pick it up as he was strolling through with a cup of coffee, read the headline, flip it over, and replace it as if it hadn't been touched. The same paper would be judiciously arranged on the coffee table in the living room by the time he returned from work in the evening. Neither his father nor he gave a second thought as to how it would have relocated. They were both working men with a job to do.

Forty minutes later at precisely 6:00 a.m., he hoisted the bag over his shoulders before trudging the mile and a half course referred to as his route.

"This is where the Schwinn could be a legitimate business expense," he reasoned to himself.

If it took him fifty-five minutes to make all the deliveries, there would only be a five-minute gap before the deadline, set according to the route manager. With the Schwinn, he was convinced the time could be cut in half. Now that would be service! Besides, Harold, the paperboy with the route adjacent to his, had a bicycle. But then again, Harold had everything. A good three inches in height, curlier brown hair, naturally straight teeth, broader shoulders, and the coveted attention from the prettiest girl in the almost junior high class scheduled to start in just two months.

Pitching one of the rolled papers onto the stoop of a red brick, two-story house with black shutters, he kicked at the rusty grate connecting the pavement of the street to the curb. He was frustrated. To him, there was more work to being a paperboy than there was reward. Time was running out. If school started without any noticeable change to distinguish himself from being a sixth grader, all his efforts would be for nothing. It didn't feel like he'd grown even a portion of an inch since he was ten. According to his orthodontist, his braces had another year before they'd be removed. And like it or not, the prettiest girl in the almost junior high had a best friend who could make his stomach do flip-flops simply by her presence.

Turning twelve also turned out to be a little more complicated then he imagined. Of course, there was still this thing about becoming a millionaire. Rounding the corner and then counting two houses that didn't subscribe to the paper, he slouched just enough for the bag to slide forward off his shoulders, over the back of his head, and then fall to the ground. It was the halfway point, the usual resting spot before continuing the journey back toward his home.

From the inside pocket of the bag, he took out the subscription booklet with sixty-five golden cards being sandwiched between black hardback coverings and held together by two silver rings. Below the customer name and address on each card were rows of half-inch perforated squares with dates printed in bold letters to be used as receipts to track payments. He flipped through it quickly, tallying the money left to be collected before the weekend. Subtracting his cost for the papers from the total, he determined there remained nine dollars and eighty-five cents of profit he could earn if everyone paid him.

Creaking as it opened, the screen door of the white Victorian house across the street - the one without a paper subscription - carefully closed behind the stranger and his dog. At first he thought they would head toward the red sports car in the driveway, but the man hesitated. He was taller than most even before putting on the black cowboy boots. His rigid posture seemed methodical, making his actions and steps appear to be moving in slow motion. Everything about his ruggedness was unfamiliar apart from a Western movie.

He stooped down to unhitch the leash from the mangy dog that then reciprocated by running down the steps and across the street to where he sat watching. As the man slowly drew closer, he couldn't help but check to see if the stranger was wearing a holster or revolver. Gunslingers often did.

Without taking his eyes from the approaching stranger or, for that matter, being aware of his reaction, he stood up from the canvas bag shuffling about, trying hastily to situate it back on his shoulders.

Just as it rested haphazardly on his left side, a gravelly voice said, "Here, let me give you a hand with that, partner." The stranger casually flipped the half-full bag of papers onto his own shoulder as if it were lighter than a woman's purse. "My friends call me Nekkers. Please to make your acquaintance, son. This grungy old bag of bones, we just call him Dog. He's a wild one, but he knows good folks when he sees them. Which direction you headed?"

Nodding kitty-corner across the street toward the next block, they walked toward the stop sign. After crossing, he took out a paper and pitched it toward the first house on their right.

"Let me give you a tip, young man. You can throw it underhanded. Like this." He flawlessly tossed the next one into the perfect spot roughly within reaching distance from where the door would swing open. "You don't have to throw it high, just smoothly. See? You try one."

Walking a few yards to the next house, he did as the man had shown him. "Wow! That is so much easier!"

"I know a thing or two about newspapers. I'm a retired muckraker."

"A what?"

"A muckraker. You'll understand if you look it up when you get home. Needless to say, I've done my share of time tossing newspapers. Started out doing just what you're doing. Can you tell me what the headline is today?"

"No, I . . . ummmm . . . haven't read it."

"You should always read the paper first before you ask folks to pay you for one."

"I don't really have time," he grumbled.

"Let me guess. Those papers come bundled. You have to sort, roll, and rubber band them before you load up your bag."

"Well ya."

"In my day, I'd roll half of the papers before I started and the rest as I walked. It gave me plenty of time beforehand for reading. Have you ever looked inside a newspaper, son?"

"No. My grandparents do though," he replied with assurance that, somehow through osmosis, his relationship earned him credibility.

Chuckling, Nekkers kept his steady, even stride as the two strolled down the street, tossing papers onto porches, stoops, and walkways. He seemed as wise as he was tall, even more perhaps. Either way, it made him feel eager to learn more.

After a couple blocks, Nekkers asked, "Come on, son. Tell me what makes you the best paperboy?"

"I'm not sure I am." He hesitated.

"Why not?"

"Well, Harold has the route next to mine. He has a bicycle and can do it in half the time."

"That won't make a hill of beans difference, my boy. Being the best is about how well you deliver the paper, not how fast. You see, none of your customers know how long it takes to do your route. What they know is how well you do it. I saw you back there, counting your payment cards. How much do you have left to collect this week?"

"About nine dollars and eighty five cents. That's if everyone pays me."

"And will they?"

"Probably not. I'm beginning to think this whole thing is rigged so the route manager can make money off my work," he complained with assumed authority.

"He does. And it's not just him, but the whole newspaper making money. And let's hope so because, if they weren't, you'd be out of a job."

"That's not fair."

"Sure it is. They call it business, my boy. Let me explain something I learned long ago. You can count your receipts every time you come around that corner, but it'll never be enough. And you can count every dime you make as a grown man and still struggle with the feeling you left money and talent on the table. You can never measure up to all the lofty goals your dreams will create until you figure out what you're working for. For me it started with how to be the best."

"Were you the best?" he asked curiously.

"No, not really. Seems there's a catch to being the best."

"What's the catch?"

"Why."

"What do you mean? Why?"

"First you have to ask yourself: why would you even want to be the best? Tell me. What do you know about it?"

"Harold is the best at everything. I'm not sure why. He just is."

"Ya, there's always a Harold in the mix, making the rest of us look good coming in second or, for that matter, last place."

"So how do I beat him?"

"You can't."

"Then why bother?"

"Because, my boy, there is more to this than beating the Harolds of the world. It's about your character. Frankly it is the one thing you do have control over. Have you ever heard folks grumbling about going to work on Monday mornings?"

"Ya, my mom and dad always start complaining about Mondays on Sunday and keep it up until Wednesday. Then they talk about hump day and Fridays."

"That's fairly common and nothing really wrong with it. But it won't make them feel like they are the best. What do you think would happen if they prepared for Mondays instead of complaining about it? Say, for instance, if instead of dreading Mondays throughout the weekend, they put a little extra time in smoothing out all the little details that cause Mondays to be hectic."

"That is sort of how I feel about rolling the papers every morning."

"So why do you do it, if you dread it?"

"Well, there's a red Schwinn bike I'm saving for. That and being a millionaire someday."

Fully tossing his head back, Nekkers laughed heartily. "Indeed! Indeed! I was one once."

"Really? A whole millionaire?"

"Sure enough. Did you see that sports car in the driveway? It's my fourth one. But can I tell you what was better than that?"

"Nothin'."

"Well actually, I'd trade in everything I have ever earned for one thing."

"Really! Trade in a million?"

"Yes, son. And then some."

"For being the best?"

"Nope, not even that. To know I did it all for Christ. Do you know who He is?"

"Ya, I learn about Him in church."

"You should pay close attention to it, my boy. He's the real deal. If you do everything as if you're doing it for Christ, you will never worry about the Harolds of the world, being best, bicycles, or even millions for that matter. It simply won't be important. Because, by the mighty, powerful, and unfathomable hand of God, you will find, instead of working toward the goal, you will already have the reward."

"I hadn't thought about doing it for Jesus. How will I know if He knows?"

"He does. Count on it. Every time, count on it. It says so in the Bible, and you'll know so every time if you read it. Then do it."

"That's my house. Do you want to come in and meet my grandmother?"

"Na, not really. I'm sure she's a great grandmother. But Dog and me, we have some muckraking to get to. Don't forget to look it up. Thanks for the stroll, son."

"Anytime. How about again tomorrow?"

"Sorry. I'm just visiting and will be leaving early in the morning. Remember what I told you. This paper route could be one of the most important things you do for yourself. See you later."

With a squeeze to the shoulder and pat on the back, Nekkers turned and walked back toward the shiny sports car. Dog chased after him. The next morning at 5:20 a.m., the thud came as expected. Rolling out of bed, he ran down the stairs, ready to read what the headline would say. When he opened the door, sitting on the top of one of the bundles was a small, brown, leather Bible.

Chapter 5: The Elevator Man

The Lord is my rock,
my fortress and my deliverer;
my God is my rock,
in whom I take refuge,
my shield and the horn of my salvation,
my stronghold.

Psalm 18:2

She waited on the two buttons, one pointed up and the other pointing down. Either could be a combination to open the heavy sliding doors and providing an exit from the corridor on the third floor of the hospital. As she stared, the dull gray behind each arrow did not convey to her brain a decision between the two was necessary to trigger her escape. Recognition, for her, went only as far as the air coming in and out of her lungs striking a chord in tandem with the punching beat. It was only her heart. It was loud.

Beneath her feet, the carpet in muted patterns of blue and brown tweed, the ceiling above with glaring florescent lighting, the windows to the left holding the sunshine out, and two identical elevators on either side flanked by six-foot Schefflera plants growing from matching copper pots all vanished from the tunnel between her pounding and the buttons. The hospital noises and smells lurked in the gap.

She had to escape before every inch of dignity exploded into the tiniest pieces of pain splattering into a humiliation she would not survive if witnessed by another soul. Without an observer, she could convince herself it didn't happen. Her son would keep the secret too.

There is something exquisitely lovely about denial. It masks the truth and comforts in ways only a down comforter brings warmth to chilled bones. Wrapped in the reassurance of privacy, the steel doors of denial could open or close as easily as elevators, if only a button were pushed to choose.

"Breathe," she told herself. *"It will come soon. It must come."*

Nothing. She continued her stare toward the buttons. Just to the right, the seam of light blue wallpaper met with its counterpart in the pattern. A tiny corner curled from the intended place of security. Would it unravel completely if she flicked at it with her fingertip? She hesitated before touching it tenderly, gently pressing it to the intended position. Again it uncurled as she withdrew her caress. A single tear quietly squeaked out from the corner of her eye. The wallpaper had been damaged too.

She heard the shuffling of feet approaching, coming from behind her and around the corner by the windows. She smeared away the tear, blinking hastily. A stranger could not see her. Not her pounding, not her anguish, and certainly not her truth. Disappearing was ultimately her choice. She hid deep inside herself in the façade of courtesy. As she shifted her weight and took nearly a slight step to the right, the man reached across from beside the left of her to push the up button. The light behind it lit in acknowledgment that a choice had indeed been made. Shaking her head in disbelief, she was embarrassed by her waiting and waiting and waiting pointlessly in her imaginary self-paralysis. After simply two exhales and then a chime notifying the stranger and her, the doors would open upon their request.

They both stepped in, he to the right and she to the left, turning to face their destination listed on either side panel of the doors as they slowly closed in front of them. The G with a matching star next to it was hers. His choice was at the top of the list, although for her it posed only as a lit button. In line with his selection, the elevator began to go up with each floor excruciatingly sounding another chime as it passed in slow motion.

"No! It was to go down!" she screamed inside herself. *"This is too long! Too far! Too much!"*

Her pounding was louder than the four walls of the elevator could hold. She closed her eyes and hung her head down.

"Breathe," she told herself. *"Just breathe."*

She rocked back and forth on each foot in an effort to feign balance. Clasping her hands together, she wrung them like a wet towel. The next chime came slowly.

"Are you okay?" he asked as he touched her arm.

The man was of average height, perhaps five-foot-ten or eleven inches. His physique matched in ordinariness. The clothing he wore, a dark polo shirt and trousers, were likewise common. His hair, gray and cut by a barber, was indistinctive. Equally so was his face. Yet his hand, wise and sympathetic, held more than a simple touch to her arm. And his voice, if it could have been, it would have been that of her father's. Her father had passed many years earlier without leaving a day where she didn't know she still needed him.

"Ya, I'm okay. Yes, I'm fine. Thank you." She heard the weakness in her words as another floor chime reminded her they were moving in the wrong direction.

"I don't mean to pry, honey. You seem upset. Can I help?" In comparison to hers, his words were strong, sturdy, and steadfast.

When the Holy Spirit swings its sword through unimaginable distance and time, someone who is weary cannot fight back. In the small confines of the walls of the elevator, she had nowhere to go except into the protective arms of the Holy Spirit. Her façade dissolved a bit.

"I'm just a little hurt. I'll be okay as soon as I get home. Thank you for asking. That is kind of you." Her eyes began to shed any pretense, and the thickening in her throat caused her to swallow hard.

"May I pray for you?" he asked.

She could only nod her head. He reached to push the stop button, took her hands in his, and prayed. *"Dear heavenly Father, You alone know what we need, when we need, where we need, and how we need. Today I thank You for this beloved sister and all the needs she will find in You. It is where Your miraculous blessings are hers, dear Lord. Quietly and in our pain, Your Word says You will find us. This I know, Father God. You are the comforter in our sorrow, the rock, the fortress, and the deliverer where we can take refuge. Please let her know Your mighty, powerful, and unfathomable hand is with her today, yesterday, tomorrow, and as always. Amen."*

"Thank you. That was beautiful," she whispered.

"What do you need, Sister?" he asked.

"I'm sorry. I wish there was something you could do to help, but you can't. Your prayer helped though. Thank you."

"Try me," he encouraged.

She trusted him for no other reason than she wanted to. It was quiet in the elevator. The world had stood still with a push of a button. This was a place where she could put everything on hold, even if only for the few minutes she needed.

"My granddaughter was born today. When I went to see her, my son asked me to leave. He is expecting his stepfather any time, and we were divorced a few weeks ago. My son doesn't want us to run into each other. So he asked me to go." She paused to gulp back her next words. "I didn't get to see her." Her hand intuitively covered her mouth as she began to sob. The words she spoke carved her pain into too much truth.

"So you left?" he asked.

She nodded her head as the warmness of tears ran down her cheeks and over the front of her hand. The sound inside her did not escape; however the pain it was hiding had.

"Go back," he said. "Call his stepfather and ask him to give you a few minutes. Then go back. Meet your granddaughter and tell her you love her. You must go back." He was so emphatic that she was not sure anyone could have refused him, and hardly an excuse would have swayed his conviction.

He pushed the button back to the third floor where they had come from. As the doors opened, he put his hand on the small of her back and guided her to the right where several arrangements of empty couches and chairs were waiting. They sat at the first one. She dialed the number and rested as it rang. He placed his hand on her shoulder as she leaned forward and down with her head hanging almost to her knees.

"Hi. I'm here at the hospital. Would you mind giving me a few minutes with the baby? I can text you when I'm leaving. It won't be long, I promise." She paused for a few moments, listening to his response. "Thank you."

She turned to the man from the elevator, "He agreed."

The man stood up as she did, facing each other. He put both hands on her shoulders, locked eyes with her, and sternly said, "Listen to me. You are her grandmother. Do not let anyone try to take that away from either of you and most importantly from her. I don't care what is going on, what your situation is, or why there is so much pain in your family. But this little girl is not a part of that. The world is a harsh place, and she needs her grandmother's love. Now go. Walk in faith. God knows what both of you need."

Then he turned her around and gently nudged her in the direction beyond the hallway where meeting her granddaughter was now determined. Before she rounded the corner to head down the corridor, she turned to look back. He was standing with his back to her in front of the elevators where the up button was again lit. Watching, she saw him lick his forefinger and begin smoothing over the curl in the corner of the wallpaper. With his touch, it stayed fixed.

Chapter 6: The Homeless Physician

On a good day, enjoy yourself;
on a bad day, examine your conscience.
God arranges for both kinds of days
so that we won't take anything for granted.

Ecclesiastics 7:14 (MSG)

After having gotten their time of arrival confused with another event later in the week, they showed up at the church a half hour earlier than originally planned. There was hardly enough time for him or his father to leave and return without then being late. Together they sat like the proverbial lumps on a log in the last pew with hands identically crossed in their laps. With no other distractions to occupy his attention, at least for the time being, he began to study the church as if dissecting it would provide the entertainment missing in their waiting. Regardless of the familiarity, his curiosity deliberated over many random pieces to a puzzle, particularly how it was first built. Who chose the colors, fixtures, windows, or cobblestone flooring? Questions began churning to deafen the quiet.

At the age of seventeen, even the most curious of young men could hardly identify their destiny, as they declared such as fact. He would go to university in a couple months and become an engineer. Within a few years of graduation, he would have a family with a beautiful, loving wife mothering their two children, a son and daughter. Sports would drive his free time, and Christ would be the center of it all. Decisions would be made according to what he learned from scripture and through prayer. Church would be the glue for their social placement. Family and old friends would always gather without question on Sunday mornings and Wednesday evenings. All would be well in his world. He was a good Christian.

In this pew with his father, who had set the example he intended to follow, he wondered if a man like him ever doubted his faith. The question was no more approachable than perhaps the answer was. Indeed the church was beautiful. The arching stained glass windows on either side were impeccably straight as they pointed heavenward. The heavy mahogany-stained woodwork of the trim, the beams curving with the ceiling, and the row upon row of pews spoke of hearty strength. The cobblestone floor replicated an ancient castle, as did the black sconces and chandeliers evenly placed to repeat the patterns set by the windows. Above them, a small balcony holding a golden pipe organ intended to scream the melody of tradition. Every detail pointed to the simple altar at the end of the three pathways, one on either side and one in the middle of two rows of pews. On the backside of the seating, brown leather-bound Bibles were evenly positioned in the brass holders with invitation cards neatly tucked next to each, most likely arranged by a faithful servant.

There were two steps up to the platform where a modest pulpit stood just slightly to the right of center. The normally scattered musical instruments with microphones, electrical cords, and accessories had all been removed for this particular occasion. In the emptiness, the wooden cross seemed to be more prominent then he had noticed in a half lifetime of visits. Simple in design, two deeply dark brown, nearly to the point of black, naturally roughed, square logs intersected where the torso and arms of Christ would have stretched. A few inches from the top, a small scroll with the Hebrew words עלה הוא ("He has Risen!") was inscribed.

Above, a massive window in the shape of a star with prisms intricately braided in patterns showcasing the streams of sunlight, as if a human craftsman could enhance what God would create on any ordinary day. All of it, every detail simple in its grandeur began to register with him for the first time.

"How I had taken it for granted," he thought.

People began to mingle as they quietly entered. Others found their usual seats while his father and he sat peacefully in the back, unmoved by the activity. Neither his mind nor heart was ready to move from discovering the beauty of the church surroundings to those of the folks gathering for the same reason he had come, to hear the speaker who would reveal an improbable journey of faith.

For him, the journey had been a solidly respectable and traditional experience. He had been born and raised in a family where his father, quietly humble in his strength, led his mother with the gentlest love. She was soft-spoken, kind, and naïvely generous without exception. Every aspect of who she was from her love, service to others, possessions, time, and spiritual gifts were given without regard to those who crossed her path. As their firstborn, he was especially favored. Imagining even a hint of a moment beyond the safety of his parents was inconceivable. Like the church, he also had the luxury of taking it for granted.

In the midst of others moving about, he felt a subtle shift within himself as something changed. It wasn't urgent, persuasive, or loud. He simply felt deeper, somehow fuller. Speaking about it seemed foolish for he hardly understood what or why anything was different from a few days earlier when he'd last been there. In the reasoning part of his mind, everything was the same. Yet in those few moments, there remained a certainty and intensity in realizing he indeed was changing.

He looked toward his father, who watched intently the very movement of people in the sanctuary he was trying to dismiss. The years had been good to his dad. He was conventionally handsome despite the small patches of gray on his temples hinting the dark hair would someday expose his youth had been spent. Only a couple inches taller, his father and he would soon look eye to eye. Dedicated to God first, his father lived a life of commitment to family. By example, it was a life spoken to those who cared to know. He worked hard, smart, and fairly in all his dealings as a businessman.

"Dad, how are you doing?"

"I'm doing well. I'm sorry I got the time mixed up. We should have stopped for dinner first."

"It's okay, Dad. I'm not really hungry yet. Maybe after?"

"Sure thing, son. I'd be pleased to buy you a meal." He chuckled.

Soon there would come a time when dinners would not be as easily synchronized, and they both knew it. It was another thing he realized he took for granted.

Nodding toward the front, his father motioned attention to the center of the church where the pastor was beginning to introduce the speaker. Standing next to him, a thin, frail, modestly dressed man with long brown hair and matching scraggly beard shifted from side to side with his hands leisurely clasped behind his back. His blue sports jacket and brown trousers seemed ill-fitting for a man in his late forties.

From the back row, he could see the man's eyes were deep, soulful, and meek. Around his neck, the only adornment he wore was a gold chain with a rugged cross identifying him as a Christian. There was no mistaking this man had not enjoyed the easiness of a journey like his own. Sadly he prayed for the ending to the man's story to be one of victory and not one of need.

Truly those who claim such through the blood of Christ often find they define victory differently. Surprisingly educated in how he articulated details, the stranger told a testimony worthy of consideration by those locked in the "taken for granted" experience the stranger had lost. His life had been charmed. He had been raised in a good family among an affluent community in Tennessee where they proudly considered themselves to be the buckle of the Bible belt. His faith, scripture, religion, and church had been an integral part of his rearing. Groomed to follow in the family tradition, he attended college with the foreknowledge he would then continue to medical school to become a physician. Blessed with the gift to learn easily, he excelled in most everything he attempted. Beyond academics, he thrived in the competition of any given sport. "I had the pick of beautiful and bright women to court. And once I made a decision to marry, she was the finest woman God created." He said with unmatched affection.

They met in medical school, encouraged each other through the trials, celebrated their successes, and soon became partners for life, blessed by God. Together they had two amazing girls who brought a dimension to his faith that would never be discovered if not through their eyes and hearts. He loved his three girls deeply with every inch of the person God created him to be. His wife was a pediatrician, and he was an orthopedic surgeon. Life had surpassed good by any man's standards. "I was living beyond my fondest desires or dreams."

Faithful to God in all of it, he knelt in gratitude every morning before he left his bedroom. He prayed over every patient, procedure, and staff person that crossed his path. He served his church and the homeless shelter and mentored young physicians struggling with addiction. He tried not to take a moment for granted.

His voice became solemn as he continued, "One fateful afternoon I was delayed in surgery. It was my evening to take the girls on our weekly date night for giggles and father-daughter memories. I phoned my wife, asking her to pick them up from school while I finished with a patient. She teased me about how she might just poach on our night to tag along. On her way home, a semi driver who had been drinking ran a red light, broadsiding them, instantly killing the three people I cherished most in this world."

"There were not enough hours in a lifetime of days to hold my grief." He continued. "I went back to work, trying in desperation to fill the void, to find a purpose and to convince myself God had a plan no one this side of eternity would understand. My patients were waiting for me."

It was more than he could manage, apart from the drugs he prescribed for himself. His addiction was soon discovered, forcing him to lose his medical license. Without an income, the house of now flimsy financial cards fell hard, leaving him facing foreclosure. "Pure, bitter shame determined how I rejected help or love from anyone else in the harshest ways I could find. The day the bank officers and a state trooper showed up to take possession of my home, I opened the door, invited them in, picked up my jacket and Bible, then walked out."

The following years were spent walking from one homeless shelter to the next, from town to town, crisscrossing the United States, each day defying God to show up with provision. Without fail He did. The crisscrossing mimicked how he questioned his faith. Many days were counted through the war he waged with God, and still others were met with exhaustion. Time marked on calendars remotely resembled restoration, despite being contradictory to his intention. He survived.

"Miraculously by the mighty, powerful, and unfathomable hand of God, I gradually found a renewed purpose for my life by spreading the Word to anyone I came in contact with. In it, I also found a deep love and gratitude for Philippians 4:4-7." Carefully he recited it.

> *Rejoice in the Lord always. I will say it again: Rejoice! Let your gentleness be evident to all. The Lord is near. Do not be anxious about anything, but in every situation, by prayer and petition, with thanksgiving, present your request to God. And the peace of God, which transcends all understanding, will guard your hearts and your minds in Christ Jesus.*

"Along the way I had been offered high-paying speaking engagements, jobs working with physicians struggling with addiction, and a variety of opportunities to move from the street. I declined them all, choosing instead to stay the course God called me to. Between God and me, I came to truly appreciate restoration would not include going back to my former life. Instead I was fully redeemed and clearly understood my mission without the slightest hint of lamenting." He ended with an encouraging prayer to seek God in all things.

The stranger's testimony was disturbing, particularly for a seventeen-year-old young man who oddly minutes earlier realized how much he took for granted, down to the smallest details of the church he loved.

"Dad, would you mind too much if we took a pass on dinner? I'd like to stay to have a word with the speaker?"

"I'll wait for you, son. Take your time. I'll meet you at the car." His father understood far more than he imagined.

While his head reeled with questions, the young man struggled to compose a single thought as he sheepishly waited for the man who was walking toward the back of the church. "Sir, how do I ...how . . . ummmm . . . I was wondering. I'm not sure, but how do I ..." He couldn't form the sentence.

"My boy, you don't have to. God will."

Something in the comforting sound of his voice brought clarity as he asked, "I've lived a life similar to yours when you were my age. My testimony is boring. Should I be worried it could all change? Or if it doesn't, my purpose won't matter?"

"Let me ask you this. How many people do you know who have testimonies similar to mine?"

"None. Most everyone I know doesn't have much to complain about. We probably take it for granted when we shouldn't."

"Exactly. I readily admit my story is unusual. If everyone had a testimony like mine, it would become ordinary. Do you think God wants the miracle of His restoration to seem commonplace?"

"No, I guess not. But how do I know it won't be me someday?"

"You don't. The most important thing you can do for yourself is prepare your relationship with God, so if it does, you will know to pick up your Bible as he calls you from safety. God wants your love, my boy. He wants you to choose Him regardless of the circumstances. Even when everything is going well."

"What confuses me is it sounded like you were faithful to God before it happened. The testimonies I've heard before have been about people who had a miserable life, were introduced to Christ, and then were healed by His grace. But it was just the opposite for you."

"God doesn't work in only one direction. And yes, I tried the best I could to be faithful. I wasn't perfect, but I loved God with my whole heart, with all of my strength, and all my mind. It wasn't a trade-off or negotiation to continue a happy life. What you should understand, my boy, is, had I not been faithful during the good times, I would not have survived the challenges. Do you understand what I'm explaining to you?"

"Before you got here, I was sitting with my dad and began to realize for the first time all the things I take for granted, starting with this church. I felt a change happen inside me, but I don't understand why. Do you think God is preparing me for something awful to happen?"

"No, I think He is revealing Himself to you. Take it slow, be patient with yourself, listen carefully, and explore what God is doing. Stay close to His Word, and you will get to know Him the way He yearns for you to know. In a unique way, He created you to know. Scripture tells us not to worry. You will find, if you open yourself up to seeing those things normally taken for granted as little miracles, you will draw closer to God."

"I have a lot to learn."

"Thankfully we all do."

"Well, I should be going. My dad's waiting for me. We're going to get dinner."

"I'm glad you stopped to talk. You are a fine young man with good questions. I'm convinced you will find the answers. God loves you, my friend. Be faithful and stay in the Word. All will be well with your soul."

With the final words, the stranger turned and walked toward the door. Only God knows where he slept that night, exactly how he preferred it to be. The father and son had dinner together, discussing the possibilities in growing from being a boy to a man of God. And the church would no longer be the same again for any of them.

Chapter 7: The Professor

Make every effort
to enter through the narrow door,
because many, I tell you,
will try to enter and will not be able to.

Luke 13:24

As she felt a warm tear slipping out onto her pillow, her eyes opened for merely a split second, and then slowly blinked back to being drowsily half closed. It was another day.

"When had waking in the morning become something one wouldn't take for granted?" she sleepily pondered.

The years and decades had strung together as if no one were counting. Now as she nestled in room 214 of the nursing home, the realization had become far more acute than at any other time in her eighty-one years. Perhaps it was the never-ending droning of sounds down the straight and narrow halls calling her to stir during the quietest times of early, early and just before daylight. Being a morning person wasn't a tag she ever aspired to become, apart from rare occasions when her appointment calendar interrupted with a call for such a commitment.

Now without any interruptions left, she found the sweet spot between slumber and awakening was the treasured part of her day - the short, fragile moments when she was aware of herself but not yet alert to the world. It was a soft time, hazy with all the comfort of being warmly wrapped in a blanket while resting her thoughts on a pillow. It became her practice to gently linger, remembering and hoping it would last just a bit longer. She found comfort in reminiscing about unspoken moments remarkably placed in the events of her life and ultimately changing her direction, even as she now waited for the one final direction that would be her last.

Today, joining her to rest on the nightstand next to her hazy awakening was a book of poems thoughtfully given as a gift from a stranger. The rough brown binding wrapped around it prompted her to drift back to a textbook from when she was a much younger woman.

"*Oh so young*," she thought, even though, at the time, she was a decade older than any of the other students.

It had been an awkward blend of desperate need and total intimidation, crafting a teeter-totter guiding her both toward and away from college.

Because she had been raised in poverty, the focus from her parents had always been on working for a living. Education was considered a luxury simply not available to her. Hearing more than her fair share of taunting messages, she believed either way, it was true. Going to college would be a waste of time and money because she simply wasn't bright enough to pass, get good grades or ever finish. She counted twenty-eight years of hearing all the reasons why not. With the rationale also came the consistent clamor played by the countdown of her parents to her eighteenth birthday when they would no longer be responsible for supporting her. As the end of her high school years wound down, the options she didn't have became clear.

Doing as expected, she married and had babies, two of them. Ironically it was her husband and his family who revealed what lay on the other side of a college graduation. With master's degrees being the norm for their family, encouragement was surprisingly abundant for her husband to continue his education after they married. Together they both worked and dreamed of a day when the burden would be lightened, providing an easier life. When he graduated she witnessed the doors being opened for him to move beyond a scarce income into the comfort he had promised through their sacrificing.

It didn't take long for him to change his mind about happily ever after with her. After finding herself on the other side of a marriage, looking into the faces of her two children, she instinctively knew she must change her inherited legacy for no other reason then for them. The paralyzing sense of being stuck was not how she wanted her children to feel about their future.

It took three attempts before she actually made it into the classroom of a small town junior college. The first effort was aborted on the day of registration shortly after she pulled into the parking lot full of other students. Despite steadying her bearings the day before with a dry run, cars and scurrying eighteen-year-olds now weighed in on her confidence as a huge block of concrete crushing her chest. That day she watched. Far different from the dry run, the hustle and bustle of others going where she was unsure to go. For an hour she watched from the last space in the back parking lot until, without getting from her car, she gave up and went home.

The following semester she tried again. Enrolled in classes for less than a week before the first one was to begin, she timidly entered the opened doors into the large hallway, not knowing which direction to go. The crowd jostled her along a route that only convinced her she didn't belong. Once the swarm of students dissipated, she sat on a bench in the hallway until no one would witness her leave.

On the third try, one year after her initial attempt, she made it through the doors, down the hallways, and into a classroom to learn English literature. The words in the textbooks, the poems, and even the rough brown binding confused her. None of it made sense or came naturally as she read and reread her first assignment.

The easygoing professor was relaxed with a casual manner as he asked the students how they interpreted the meaning of an assigned poem. He called on several who were ready to burst forth with confident intellect as they imparted words of wisdom spoken with a command of the lesson she didn't recognize. As she fervently flipped the pages of her book to compare what they said with the assignment, her sense of dread returned.

"*Had she read the wrong material? What were they talking about? Where did it say anything near that? How could she be so out of place again?*" she thought.

While wandering aimlessly among the desks, the look on her face must have alerted the professor to her confusion, which then prompted him to ask for her thoughts. Even if she were certain about the answer, remaining invisible held more assurance for her. Not to talk. It was too late to escape. She was trapped.

"Ummmm, I think ...well . . .I'm not sure ... but I ahhh might have read the wrong assignment." She died inside.

"Go ahead. Give it a try," he encouraged.

She didn't recognize where the answer came from - not the thoughts, the opinion, or even the language she used to explain it. The word "metaphor" had not crossed her lips, let alone found its way into a meaningful sentence. The poem remained foggy to her, and she hadn't remembered it in enough detail for interpretation for the class. Her answer was foreign to what the others had conveyed, and she believed it certainly must have been wrong. She was embarrassed. Despite everything, the professor triumphantly told the class, "You are actually the only one who has gotten it correct."

Seeing the faces of the other students, she felt sadness replace her panic. The last thing she wanted was for anyone to feel he or she was wrong or not smart enough to figure it out. Everything inside her believed getting it right was a fluke, and she wasn't convinced it would ever happen again. To her, comfortable would have been being right about being wrong.

Her head was still buzzing when the class ended, and she hurriedly headed for the door. Deep inside her own anguish, she failed to notice the professor approaching the door as she did, bumping into him as he reached for the knob. Readjusting, he reached his arm above her head to hold the door open. She walked under.

Alongside her steps, he said, "You know you are very bright. I'm convinced you will do well at anything you put your mind to, including college."

There, as she walked from her world of self-doubt into the next world of accomplishments, was a stranger who spoke two sentences that impacted the rest of her life. If metaphors are real, his holding the door open was an invitation to cross to the other side by way of the bridge he built with his words. He had faith in her, and she believed him. For the next fifty-three years, she believed him.

When self-doubt crept in, she believed him. When the world told her she couldn't, she believed him. When her past tried to dim her future, she believed him. The years flew by full of twists and turns, successes and failures, love and heartbreak. When those seemingly endless feelings tried to repeat in the same vein as her three attempts to go to college, she believed him. For the hand used to reach for the door was not his. But instead it was the mighty, powerful, and unfathomable hand of God.

As the light from the sun became brighter in room 214, the noise down the hall drew closer with sounds of others starting their day. She wondered about the professor, the students she never knew, or perhaps bridges she may have unknowingly built with her own words. She wondered about the sacrifices of time and money to accomplish her goal, when the value of it came so subtly in a brief moment.

Another tear dropped to her pillow when she quietly understood the professor probably walked away without realizing how he changed the direction of her life.

And then finally, she recognized how cherished it is to know. There was so much she could no longer remember. She stared at the book on her nightstand, wanting to recall the stranger who left it behind. Slipping her hand out from under the covers, she reached for it. Her hand looked unrecognizable and odd. It was wrinkled, twisted, and old. The nails were unpainted, and the thinness of her skin seemed as sheer as her memory. Her grip was weak as the book slipped from her frail fingers, landing next to her shoulder. She saw a piece of blue parchment falling from the book. Words were scrawled in a familiar script.

> "Brains and beauty ... what more could a man ever ask for? I love you, sweetheart!"
>
> Charles

"Do I know a Charles?" she wondered.

Chapter 8: The Millionaire

For I, the Lord, love justice;
I hate robbery and wrongdoing.
In my faithfulness
I will reward my people
and make an everlasting covenant with them.

Isaiah 61:8

If you were to see her walk past, you'd never guess she was a millionaire. She was not a conventional one or even a lucky one. She didn't make, win, or inherit the money. She simply accepted it very unexpectedly on a rather normal day. And yes, it changed her life, although not in the ways you'd think. In subtly indescribable ways, any before and after pictures of her would look vaguely different. You wouldn't be able to put your finger on it, wondering perhaps if it were the lighting or maybe she'd gotten a good night's sleep. Either way something in her appearance was decidedly different. But you'd hardly be able to define it.

She refused to give her name the day she called to set an appointment with an attorney for a divorce. It frightened her that someone may leak the information to her husband. All the attorney/client privilege in the world wasn't enough to ease her apprehension. Nor was the truth. No one really cared enough to remember or repeat the information. So on the calendar, her appointment was labeled "The Frightened Woman (Divorce) Unknown Number." Normally no one in the law firm would have set an appointment if the potential client weren't prepared to follow the processes in place to protect everyone, which certainly included sharing his or her name when setting it.

After speaking with her for a few moments, something in the paralegal's gut told her to bend the rules this one time. It wasn't a knotted feeling, but a soft, warm, comforting sense, terribly unusual for her to experience, particularly in view of the fact she was especially familiar with how making tough decisions were the name of the game every day.

Truly the feeling in her stomach should have been as easy to ignore as the hundreds of prior calls mirroring the frightened woman's. Knowing the office procedures well, the paralegal still could not fathom what prompted her to set the appointment. Nor could she explain why, years later, the voice of the frightened woman eloquently lingered within the memories of their first conversation as if still speaking on the phone for the first time. Her delicate voice was timid, as close to humming one can be without a song to accompany it.

Curiosity moved the paralegal to loiter near the reception area the morning the frightened woman was expected to arrive. Answering a telephone call, the girl at the front desk asked if there were a place other than the reception area for the frightened woman to wait, as she was concerned someone might see her.

Rolling her eyes before answering, the paralegal replied, "Sure, tell her she can wait in the conference room, I suppose."

Not liking the idea, she questioned whether indeed a can of worms had just been opened.

Within a few moments, the frightened woman sheepishly materialized. She followed the lead of the paralegal to a safe haven where an intake form listing a variety of questions to be answered would serve to be the next obstacle. The frightened woman filled out only the responses she cared to share, nervously selecting information carefully. She was tiny, frail with shoulders rounded forward for protection. Her curly brown hair, cut short in a haphazard fashion, left places of unevenness as proof it had not been styled in a beauty salon. Her skin was flawlessly clean from any hint of cosmetics, and her eyes diverted every attempt to make connection with the world. The clothing she wore was well-pressed in an effort to revive any long-lost newness. A white, button-down, cotton blouse ruled with thin black stripes was turned up at the wrist, disguising the sleeve length was longer than her arms. The pair of black polyester trousers hung on her frame just as they would a hanger void of any form or fit, while squarely brushing against the unadorned flats she wore on her feet. Equally unremarkable as her appearance was the thin gold band on her left hand, the only jewelry she wore.

There was a desolate reality in the way the frightened woman grasped for dignity through the barriers of fear. It wasn't pity or sadness the paralegal felt for her. Rather instead it was a kinship learned from bygone experiences. Intentionally stored in the past, yet not completely forgotten, her role as a sister was now permitted to persist only within the haziness of memories. And she hoped hers wasn't noticeable in the same way the grappling was for the frightened woman. Even as the paralegal recognized the resemblances, she didn't want to lower her well-groomed facade to reveal any hint of empathy. Not so soon anyway.

Biding time before the attorney came for the frightened woman, they very briefly and politely spoke about the weather. She was apparently well-educated, poised, and almost resolute in contradiction to her appearance or behavior. The paralegal wondered what the details of her story would reveal or if she were prepared for the candid bluntness the attorney would no doubt convey.

Considering the hesitancy of the frightened woman, it was somewhat surprising to the paralegal that she hired the attorney during the first appointment. Then after learning many of the specifics, the paralegal didn't ask but often wondered how the retainer was afforded. During thirty-five years of marriage, the frightened woman's husband gave her sixty dollars a week to provide all the necessities for their family of four. It included clothing, groceries, gasoline, supplies, and any unexpected expenses. Her children were now grown. Sadly her daughter had moved on with her life. And equally as sad was her son had not. As an executive for a large corporation, he continued to live at home with his parents. The son was also a sidekick in delivering the harsh antics of his father as they both disregarded the frightened woman.

Remarkably, she was slow to confide about her situation. However, her husband and son had rather cruel expectations for her. For instance, if she made the wrong meal for dinner, they would throw the plate of food in the garbage, demanding she make another one. The rationale given as to why the frightened woman wasn't allowed to have friends or hold a job outside the home was quite clear. Either would distract from duties she owed to the men in her household.

To preserve her equilibrium, she became a ferocious reader, loving anything written during former eras in history. Oddly enough, considering how bright she seemed, the frightened woman had absolutely no idea where her husband worked or what he did for a living. He was a private man, she explained. The paralegal conceded she must have been a victim of her own kindness.

In an effort to provide for herself during the divorce proceedings, the frightened woman took a part-time job working as a secretary for the church she attended. Soon after she moved out of her home taking literally nothing. All indications pointed to someone from her church helping prearrange an exit, even as it was never spoken about.

The discovery phase was lengthy and grueling as her husband and his attorney were reluctant to disclose the financial information regarding the marital estate she was entitled to under the law. After months of legal maneuvering, he was forced to comply. It was the afternoon the attorney reviewed the documents when the flurry of his adding machine running numbers could be heard echoing throughout the office.

"This can't be right," he said, adding the numbers again and again until convinced.

Her portion of the marital assets was $1.75 million. The frightened woman who had been locked away from the world was married to a very successful businessman. He knew how to make others wealthy and had done so for himself as well. Family law attorneys rarely have the opportunity to take a client from such oppressive poverty to prosperity.

Walking out of the office the day she learned the truth about her situation, the frightened woman simply and humbly said, "Thank you."

There was nothing easy about enforcing the legal obligation of someone who had committed three and a half decades to conceal his wealth, but it could be done. Through many months knowing the truth and living a meager existence, the frightened woman was gentle and calm, showing no sign of fretfulness. She would wait for it to come without urgency or compulsion. And so it did.

The husband's side of the story no doubt sounded something like the typical version often suggesting she took him for everything he had. Or he worked hard for the money she had not done anything to deserve. And yet, imagining how long those thirty-five years must have been as she lived a stark, lonely life worn by the vows she made to her husband and God, could easily turn to bitterness for most anyone. Or consider how troubling it must have been for her to take the first steps out into the light. There was not a single hint her love, joy, peace, patience, kindness, goodness, faithfulness, gentleness, or self-control ever changed.

Very unceremoniously a check came delivered by a courier, addressed to her. When she came to pick it up, she spoke of how grateful she was for the kindness shown when she first called to set an appointment. For she believed it had been by the mighty, powerful, and unfathomable hand of God that it wasn't the last call she made before taking an overdose of sleeping pills.

Almost a year later, the paralegal ran into her at a hairdresser's salon. The millionaire stood a bit taller and had a lovely modest hairstyle. She was wearing just a hint of cosmetics and dressed much like their first visit, only with a bit more polish. The relationship with her daughter had been renewed, spending time together as best friends do. Neither spoke of her son.

Out of curiosity, the paralegal asked, "Have you done anything to splurge or treat yourself to something special?"

She had. "After buying a small condo close to my church, I found a vintage Steinway grand piano, had it restored, and now play it every day. Often my daughter joins me in duets."

Hanging softly around her neck, she wore a simple gold necklace scrolled in the letters J-O-Y.

Chapter 9: The Rush Hour Woman

Beloved, let us love one another,
for love is from God,
and everyone who loves
is born of God and knows God.

1 John 4:7 (NKJV)

If she were asked to defend motives for traveling faster than the speed limit, she could. "Easily," she might add with conviction. Regardless her logic would be misplaced. The wearisome and unpredictable forty-minute drive to work, some days finished within thirty-eight and a half; other days it turned into forty-four. Invariably a dreary tension was created before she left the house, whether it was the extra five minutes she slept or ironing the second dress after changing her mind on what to wear. The fact was, her dawdling had little bearing on the matter as she eked out every last second procrastinating before charging into the very traffic she blamed for any delays. Thus began the game of "beat the clock." Her GPS said it should take thirty-two minutes. And she wondered if, when calculating the glaring number it set in stone, equal consideration was given for congestion during rush hour, red traffic lights, or slow pokes driving under the speed limit. Perhaps she was simply foolish to believe in the accuracy of the GPS.

However late she arrived, within only a few minutes of being expected, someone would be tapping a toe and counting. The typical power and control game that feeble managers used to prop up their authority nevertheless struck her as immature and nonsensical. Inevitably the tapping prompted questions she didn't ask but often thought. *"Could the minutes she stayed beyond the 5:00 p.m. checkout the day before be banked for the next morning's arrival?"* It was petty and hardly warranted the additional importance it produced. Nonetheless, she played the game as an accomplished champion.

An ever-fluctuating strategic plan was put in place each day as she moved through traffic, contemplating which lane to be in at every juncture, calculating interference based on reading the patterns of fellow drivers, and skirting around well-worn interstates by way of a less traveled route all in an effort to improve her ultimate outcome. Could she beat the clock? Within the mapped out strategy lay an unguarded two-mile street in a quiet neighborhood. With one stop sign at the midpoint and another at the end, there was virtually no traffic. It proved to be a straight shot between two busy thoroughfares, where, each time she raced from one end to the other, she consistently scored a couple magic minutes back. She normally wouldn't admit it, but frequently the unguarded street effortlessly secured the difference between a waiting toe tapper and victory.

One particular day, with a beautiful sun shining behind several billowy clouds sprinkled for accent in a blue sky, the temperatures were warm but not hot. Flowers were beginning to bloom with no chance of rain. In fact it was a perfect day for a walk, if the bell weren't tolling for her to continue the thirty-two minutes from where she'd started. So without giving any of it a single thought, she rushed.

She absolutely rushed past an elderly woman walking her rumpled dog on the side of the unguarded street. There were no sidewalks, leaving pedestrians to share the space with nonchalant drivers, precisely as the woman had done however many times without being noticed. Tiny in stature, she was casually dressed with her short, gray grandma hair tightly styled about her face. She donned a big pair of sunglasses most likely left over from the Jackie Kennedy era.

A hasty glance toward the woman may undoubtedly be reminiscent of the greeting card character, Maxine, including her little dog. Any concentration she harbored in her strategic plan was impeccably broken when the woman stopped and very demonstratively planted her hands on her small hips, intently scrutinizing the silver Honda rushing past.

With the woman's reflection menacing in her rearview mirror, flying thoughts of agitation dashed in her head as she continued hurrying. "*What was up with that cranky old woman, upset about drivers speeding through a precious neighborhood as she walked her little dog during rush hour of all times?*" To make matters worse, the woman was clueless about almost getting in her way. She had to get to work. And so she did, ignoring the woman and her dog in the process.

The next day was hardly distinguishable from the previous as she continued her pattern rounding the corner, headed for the magic minutes again. In the distance, probably an eighth of a mile or so ahead, she saw the woman walking in much the same place as the day before. With only a split second to register any consideration of actually slowing down, she took her foot off the gas, coasting even as she persisted faster than the posted speed limit. Again the woman stopped, put both hands on her hips, and watched.

Unexpectedly, at the precise moment she passed, the woman raised her left hand and began to wave. It startled her. Similar to an uncontrolled bounce of a knee after a doctor taps it with a small reflex hammer is exactly how she returned the gesture. It was not a full-fledged wave, nothing of the sort. It was more of a dismissive flit of the wrist, easily reminding anyone of the reaction of a bouncing knee.

Exploding across the face of the woman, a huge smile half hidden behind her big sunglasses was sure to stop the world, if not her. The smile traveled faster than she did. Speeding from the woman's peculiar stance, through the window of a silver Honda and then settled in her place of curiosity.

Before she arrived at work, several variations of who the woman might be replaced the angst of traveling against time. *"Could she be a demented old fool wandering the streets in a manic form of existence as she faced her final days? Or perhaps she was the neighborhood gossip, tallying speeding cars just as well as feeble managers counted minutes. Had the woman been responsible for the nonconforming signs placed sporadically along the way, warning drivers of reduced speed limits and children playing? Possibly she was a retired greeting card character with a narcissistic sense of humor ridiculing the bane of civilization. Then again it was entirely feasible she was simply a cantankerous old woman missing the comfort of nagging her deceased husband and childhood friends, triggering her to become an unofficial traffic cop in their absence."*

In any event, walking into the office exchanged one set of mental gymnastics for another. She left any thought of the woman on the side of the unguarded street until the next morning when she turned to the familiar corner, remembering the smile once again.

Oddly enough, she slowed to the speed limit, searching to see if the woman was walking her dog, and indeed she was. Even stranger, she lifted the sunglasses from her own face and rested them on the top of her head. Leisurely driving, she tossed a full-face smile and waved with an enthusiasm reserved for old friends. The woman, pausing, returned the gesture in kind. Thus began a ritual they shared for several weeks. An agreement had been forged. In exchange for her slowing down, they would trade morning waves and cheerful smiles set aside for a little place and time during the hurried part of the day while toe tappers counted.

She began to look forward to the woman's greeting, often wondering about her even before she came to the turn. It was the same every day. And every day she drove by, feeling just a little more lighthearted and kind, regardless of whom the woman was. She enjoyed daydreaming about her. Doing so crafted a reassuring sense of belonging as the unguarded street transformed from a point to gain a couple minutes against the clock to the familiar face of an unknown friend. As things at work became more stressful, she carried the woman's smile and wave into the day with her. There were times the memory of it helped improve how she felt when grappling with troubling conduct from coworkers.

Inevitably the day arrived when she turned the familiar corner to find the woman was missing from the unguarded street. Alarm bells surrounded her as she frantically checked the very clock she was trying to beat for a snippet of proof her timing was out of sync. Sluggishly, well below the speed limit, she crept in slow motion, looking down the side streets, searching to confirm the woman wasn't lingering behind. She worried something dreadful happened to prevent the woman from walking her dog.

"Had she fallen? Did she have a heart attack or stroke, landing her in the hospital?" she pondered.

She searched each house for any hint it was the one the woman called home. Nothing.

Before she made her way to the end of the unguarded street, a powerful and frightening realization landed. "*What if the woman died before I'd spoken to her?*"

She couldn't count how many weeks of sharing waves and smiles they shared without speaking a single word or simply exchanging a name to utter when thanking God for His mighty, powerful, and unfathomable hand in their mornings.

The stop sign urging her to turn away also spelled regret. Fumbling through her emotions, she prayed for the woman. The sense of dread was impossible to shake, prompting her to later write a couple lines honoring how the woman inspired her mornings to post on Facebook. They were simple words. Fortunately no one responded or seemed to notice. For her it was personal. Her attempt to portray the woman as a tangible person was meager in comparison to the impact she had. Yet she felt compelled to try, just in case she wouldn't be walking her dog the next morning. Thankfully she was.

Not needing a second prompt, as she drew closer to the woman, she paused and rolled down her window to say hello. She had no idea how the woman would respond, if she would be kind or a bit cranky or if stopping would frighten her. Losing her composure a bit, she began babbling how worried she had become after missing her the day before.

The woman's voice, delicate and tender, gently explained, "Some days are just too hard for me to get out."

Her demeanor conveyed an impression of a lifetime devoted to well-bred manners and poise. Maybe it was peace or joy. Maybe she had seen far too much life to be cranky. No matter the cause, her kindness unfolded through the open window of the silver Honda as if it had been waiting all along. She felt an earnestness to touch the woman's heart, establish how important she was to her, and genuinely accept the kindness offered.

Continuing to stumble over her words, she admitted to the posting on Facebook. The jumbled awkwardness of those first words also seemed to imply a sense she may have startled the woman until she revealed what she had written. "Sometimes if you slow down you can see a touch of love coming your way."

The woman took off her own sunglasses, revealing beautiful, wise eyes leaning in even closer as she remarkably and softly answered, "Honey, love is all around you. All you have to do is look, and you will surely see it."

Do you want to know what love did that day? It fell instantly and forever for the sweetest soul who walked her little dog. Thus began a new ritual and courtship of stopping to share brief but loving words. They spoke of wearing the same shade of pink on the same day and how they liked each other's hair, the weather, and flowers. Eventually they exchanged names. The woman was Joyce, and her dog was Ozzie.

There are so many reasons the world would tell you to be suspicious of each other, to rush past an intimate exchange with a stranger, or to intently keep focused toward your destiny to avoid interruptions. And on some levels, the world may be right. But the world is not love. It amazed her, when against all the twirling activities of her own life, an unexpected breakthrough happened. Very quietly and unceremoniously, without a spotlight or grand gesture, a miracle bloomed. Instinctually she knew the two-mile section of her journey was magic. But she hardly understood the nature of it until Joyce and Ozzie.

The job didn't go well, and soon she found another one where toe tappers didn't count minutes. She was so ready to move on. The decision was easy because nothing held her there -not kindness, wisdom, friendliness, or love. It was a cold place where gossipers fed the life of discontent.

On her last day, she drove to work with an excitement strictly afforded from the release of a bad situation. As she rounded the corner toward Joyce and Ozzie, the excitement was suspended for a few minutes. She explained, "I've taken another job and won't be coming this direction in the mornings any longer."

Joyce asked. "I am so pleased, congratulations! Is it a good opportunity? You will do well, I'm convinced of it." They were both sad.

As God's version of serendipity would have it, a dentist appointment a few weeks later presented an occasion to travel the much-loved unguarded street. And yes, Joyce and Ozzie were walking. Delighted to see each other again, they enthusiastically exchanged warm greetings. She told Joyce how much she loved her new job. As was her nature, Joyce's kindness answered how happy she was to hear it. Together they chattered about unimportant things, including Ozzie's little adventure with a new collar.

With their parting words, she felt her eyes begin to tear up. Much like the first day when she babbled about not seeing her, the words tumbled out. "I've missed you."

"I've missed you too, sweetie. Just always remember you are loved."

She blew Joyce a kiss through the open window, pulled away, and watched in her rearview mirror as Joyce waved from the side of the street. Her hand was still in the air when she came to the stop sign where she would turn onto the busy thoroughfare. She loved her!

Seven months later, she chose to take the same magic route, albeit to another destination and later in the day. She was on the phone comparing notes about the neighborhood with a friend who had previously lived nearby. As the familiarity of Joyce and Ozzie drew closer, she told him of a lovely woman she had long since said good-bye to. It was a joyful story turning to wonderment as she topped the hill.

In the distance she could see Joyce walking Ozzie. Neither could believe the oddity of their conversation colliding with timing and chance again.

Chapter 10: The Fast Food Man

The King will reply,
'Truly I tell you,
whatever you did for one of the least
of these brothers and sisters of mine,
you did for me.'

Matthew 25:40

The double lines to the drive-thru window were beginning to wrap around the building as he pulled into the parking lot. He wasn't in a hurry as much as reluctant to play the mosh pit game of chase, for a simple cup of coffee. Kicking himself for not taking the extra five minutes to prepare one before he left the house, he pulled into a space just a few yards from the door and walked toward it.

Sitting on the curb next to the entrance with his head resting atop his knees was a man who obviously didn't come for the drive-thru either. His scraggly brown hair was matted in areas that may have been pressed together by dirt, sweat, and perhaps other ingredients one wouldn't want to know. Appearing to have been dipped in dirt, his shirt was a dark gray or maybe green and covered by an unseasonably heavy black coat with a hood half torn from the collar. One of the knees to his brown trousers had also been ripped, and blotches of colors smeared on the pant leg were hard to distinguish apart from being soiled. There was no doubt his black boots were worn well beyond what a reasonable person would, even as they looked far bigger than a man of his slight build would wear comfortably.

Watching the man carefully as he walked toward the door, without lifting his head, the man reached out a red knit cap, asking for some spare change. His long fingernails were outlined in black soot, and he smelled worse than a New Orleans gutter after a long night of celebration. Curiosity got the best of him, as he looked directly at the man, eye to eye. They were dark, sullen, and more distant than what he imagined their two lives must be. The directness of the eye contact upset the man, prompting him to look away to his left side as if something had grabbed his attention. Following the man's gaze, he found nothing. Looking back, he could almost feel the heaviness of the man's shame marking the ruggedness in a desperate face. On his right cheek, a scar cut from just in front of his ear down and shy of his top lip.

"*The man needed a drink,*" he thought.

Stepping past the man into the restaurant, he stood in line behind two others, waiting to place his order. Just enough time clicked by to draw attention back to the man. Staring over his own shoulder, he saw the man was again hiding his face between his knees, clasping the empty cap in his hands as they cupped above his head.

"*It was a barrier to any onlookers, like myself,*" he thought. "*I can't imagine.*"

He ordered his coffee, black no sugar, with a hamburger, chicken sandwich, two orders of french fries, a large Coke, and a three-pack of cookies. Taking them over to the booth closest to the door, he laid the tray of food on the far side of the table facing the outside and turned back toward the man.

Holding the door open, he asked, "Hey, are you hungry? Would you care to share a meal with me?"

Surprised, the man looked back over his left shoulder, gruffly asking, "You talkin' ta me?"

"Sure. Would you like to join me?"

The man bounced up from his place on the curb, as if he'd been waiting for someone to hoist him from an imaginary trampoline. Sliding into the other side of the booth, the man began to fidget with anxiety over the price the meal would cost.

"I don' hab no moneys," he said.

"I know. It's okay. We don't want the food to go to waste, do we?" Pushing the tray of food closer toward the man, he kept the coffee and cookies on his side of the table.

"Do yuse mine if I says some werds fore I be eatin'?"

Expecting the man was going to tell a hard luck story about how he got there or why the food was well deserved, he answered, "No, go right ahead."

Instead the man bowed his head, folded his hands together, and whispered a prayer so quietly that no one could hear what he was saying until the final word, "Amens."

As he was taking the first bite from the hamburger, it was evident the man didn't have all his teeth. The first sandwich was eaten as fast as inhaling could oblige. After a few french fries and two gulps from the drink, the man began to slow down with the chicken sandwich.

"How long has it been since you've eaten?"

"Don rilly member, sir. Truly grateful yuse fed me."

"Do you live around here?"

"No, sir. I bin walkin' fur a spell."

"Where did you come from?"

"No wears."

He didn't get the impression the man was being evasive as much as not exactly knowing the answer. It struck him how easy it is to lose track of days when on vacation. If the man's life were simply a journey walking from one place to another, without the interference of other distraction, losing track of location could easily be possible. Or not.

"I ain't no drunk, sir. Not had a drop fur a long spell."

"Do you know where you'll be staying tonight?"

"Bin lookin' fur a church. Needs to git some prayins done. Yuse knows like in da holy way. Kine a thinks better when I doos."

"What do you think about the shelter downtown?"

"Cain't be getting' der, sir. Too fur frum da highways. Me's gots to stey close to da roads."

"They have a chapel. What if I can get you a ride and promise to get you a ride back when you're ready?"

"Suppose dat weren't too bad. What wilst dey want me to doos?"

"I'm not really sure. But I know they won't let you drink."

"Das aw right wits me, sir, cuz I ain't no drunk. Jist a little down on me luck is all."

Even though he felt safe eating with the man in the restaurant, he didn't want to chance anything by getting in a car together. Calling a colleague who worked with the homeless, he explained meeting a new friend who needed a ride to the shelter downtown. The colleague was happy to oblige, saying it would take a few minutes before he could be there.

While the man was eating and talking, he congratulated himself for being so patient in listening, a righteous virtue. Unlike the man, he had made better choices, accomplished honorable achievements, and was now in a position to give back. Everything about his life was in order, protected by God.

"I have sincerely earned the position I hold in a worldly kingdom." He thought.

The other man knew better. Yet it didn't stop him from becoming more animated with each sentence. An audience of one was drawn in, now beholden to listen if not hear.

The man continued to talk, mostly about being a Christ follower and asking if he were too. In his uneducated English, the man retold an incredibly eloquent story of Christ's life. His eyes were no longer dark, and the distance in them was replaced with light. His grimy hands expressed his amazement with each twist and turn, reporting how Christ performed miracles.

At the perfect point, the man abruptly stood up next to their table and asked, "Sir, if I may?"

Bowing first, he then recited the Sermon on the Mount. Sitting back down, he slowed his rhythm as he described the crucifixion in grueling specifics. The man confided about wishing he too had been at the cross with the women when Christ was crucified. He was convinced he would have stayed, for the women needed a man like him, he explained.

The stories the man told were much like those he had learned from ministers over the course of his life. Beyond hearing sermons, he had read and studied them in depth. Yet nowhere in what he learned had a rendition been delivered quite like this man could with a passionate intimacy. He pictured the man actually living each story as the recipient of the very miracles he described being performed. He believed, lived, and preached them. When the man came to the point where Christ ascended into heaven, he explained it was his purpose for being there.

"Der jus ain't no man 'live as bless'd as me! I gets to walk dis earth tellin' folks 'bout how gewd God is alls de days of me life. Do yuse knows what de bist verse in da gewd Book is? 'And God said, 'Let there be light.' And there was light.' If yuse gits dese first werds of God, yuse gits de whole messige."

Through the window he could see the colleague had arrived and was parking the car. He knew their time would end shortly. Quite unexpectedly he became anxious about the man leaving. He wasn't ready to see him go.

Fumbling for the perfect words, he asked, "Would you like the cookies to take with you?"

"Naw, me thinks yuse be needin' dem more din me. It's okay, nice man. I knows yuse ginna be jis fine. I be prayin' fer ya."

With those kind words, the man was introduced to the colleague, ready to give him a ride to the shelter. In saying good-bye, the man reached to shake his hand. Instead he kissed it, winked, and walked out the door and across the parking lot into the waiting car. As he dropped his head in prayer, there weren't words, simply emotions only God could decipher. He loved the man.

Standing next to the table waiting for his attention was one of the uniformed employees he had noticed when ordering the meal. He was young, perhaps sixteen years old, tall and thin with a pimply face and brown hair that matched his trousers.

"Excuse me," he said. "I'm sorry to disturb you, but I wanted to thank you for helping the old man. He has been coming here for the last three days and just sitting on the curb. People have been pretty cruel to him. Our manager told us if anyone fed him, we would be fired. We couldn't take it anymore, so this morning a bunch of us went into the freezer and prayed for someone to help him. We trusted God in believing they would come, and you did."

It seems by the mighty, powerful, and unfathomable hand of God all the prayers for this hungry man reached beyond answering his need for food, but also for those in the circle of life who were also praying for him. Not simply the employees, but many others who had crossed the man's path. Certainly he could count himself as part of the circle. He began to intentionally and humbly read the Sermon on the Mount at the beginning of each day, knowing the love the man shared for Christ was as righteous as any purpose.

Chapter 11: The Marathon Woman

For we walk by faith, not by sight.

2 Corinthians 5:7(NKJV)

There is no doubt, if you have a girlfriend who is a runner, if you are rattling around a spell of the blues a bit longer than normal, and if there is a marathon in San Francisco, you might just end up crossing a finish line you could not fathom. To say the least, the girlfriend's unlikely invitation to join marathon training, was intentionally understated.

"It will be fun! We can raise money for a charity, train with a group, and go to San Francisco in October."

Counting forward, there were four and a half months to transform from a physical disaster to a victorious marathoner. Saying her girlfriend could hear hesitancy in her silence was also an intentional understatement.

"We can have coffee every Saturday morning after training!" she continued.

Despite the invitation sounding more like idiocy, she agreed, but not because she had the least interest in training or for that matter doing a marathon. Saturday mornings with her girlfriend would be even richer than the much-coveted coffee. Her girlfriend was the quintessential blend of small town Southern charm and Vermont savvy wrapped in a rare beauty. With passions flowing peacefully deep into faith, family, and friends, the girlfriend was also a pottery artist.

Despite being admonished that there was no such word as "potterist," she remained lovingly nicknamed, for the pieces created were almost as lovely as she was, deserving a unique label.

Running was part of her girlfriend's day, often wedged between other passions. She would kick on a pair of shoes, and off she ran for six or seven miles through neighborhoods or in a quiet countryside. Hidden within the invitation was a dream her girlfriend carried to run a full marathon, 26.2 miles. Halves she had done many times, making this a challenge for both of them.

Contrary to her girlfriend, she was still basking in a residual year after surviving a serious health battle leaving her weakened physically, emotionally, and spiritually. It had been bad, really really bad. Through the battle to beat the illness, she sacrificed being in the best physical shape of her life, her hope and enthusiasm for the future, as well as an otherwise untested faith in God. The cocktail of medications she took for nearly twelve months came with many side effects. The one glaring in the mirror was weight gain, fifty pounds of reasons why training for a marathon was a bad idea.

Her girlfriend didn't think so.

Always with an outreached hand, her girlfriend had witnessed the downward transformation of a friend into a dark, defeated place. It wasn't simply about weight gain. It was about losing her place in life. Dominos fall hard sometimes. This time they left her waking in the morning, more times than not, crying before she opened her eyes. She had only recently confided to her girlfriend how relentless the effort to put one foot in front of the other had become. For the first time, she saw worry in her girlfriend's eyes as she grappled for words to force the dominos back into their rightful place. She would never know how the confidence traveled from her confession to a point where the invitation was extended and feared to ask.

The irony of putting one foot in front of the other, twisted into training to walk a half marathon didn't escape her. The compromise to walk a half marathon rather than run a full, combined with a worthy charitable cause and a tempting destination, all appeared doable, if not enticing at the time. The two of them were on different journeys along the same path, facing an inevitable fork in the road where they would be steered apart and then back together in the end.

Saturday mornings at 5:00 a.m., they met fellow teammates to face the interval training goals set for a particular week. The charitable organization provided a dedicated marathon coach, fund-raising partner, and a personal mentor. The game plan was in place as camaraderie bloomed. Her teammates were confident she could accomplish this, even as she remained skeptical. Doubtful enough that on the first rainy morning she explained to her girlfriend she would be happy to go to the starting point and then slip away to wait in the coffee shop until they finished.

Unbeknownst to her, the coach and mentor were duly prepared for such a proposal. She learned two things that particular rainy morning. As crazy as it seemed, walking in the rain could be refreshing, and she could face, then overcome obstacles she hadn't considered.

While commitment to the weekly training with her team continued without interruption, the daily assignments to walk the specified durations on her own were flimsy. Some days she would cooperate; other times she wouldn't. It became more and more difficult to escape them as donations from her fund-raising efforts began adding up. No longer was it simply about disappointing her girlfriend or even herself. She now had a growing audience championing her on to San Francisco to reach the goal.

A point came when she realized to join the Saturday morning training, she would have to put in the daily interval work first. As cliché as it sounded, training fueled the transformation toward accomplishing one daily step at a time for her. The idea of looking forward to the marathon was bigger than she bargained for, and she knew it. From time to time as she drove, she clocked 13.1 miles to determine how long the distance would truly be. With it came a very insidious voice in the back of her head, squeaking she wouldn't actually make the trip. However, there is also something subtly powerful about being the first person to pull into the parking lot of a gym before sunrise. And as such, the teeter-totter between both regularly restricted her view of each.

Training isn't simply about how far you travel. It also is about learning the optimum form and technique, maintaining and pacing for the duration, replenishing nutrients with fuel and electrolytes, and ultimately breaking through the psychological wall every marathoner will face sooner or later. She went from walking three miles to five miles, eight miles, and to eventually the twelve-mile mark

Twelve miles came with a confidence for her to tackle six miles in and six miles out in a beautifully wooded park. What she didn't realize was how rigorous the trail would be. The first six miles were a series of uphill climbs with a bend in the distance coaxing her to endure until she imagined relief. Uphill and then uphill again until the next uphill, and then it would repeat again and again. Yes, it was beautiful, grueling without a doubt, and in some ways vaguely familiar as her own life's pattern. Each time she thought she reached the top, she found another ascending trail beckoning with a new path to the next upward destination hidden behind a curve.

Upon reaching the summit, she rested for a few minutes. Looking over a park bench positioned between rows of trees, she was able to see hills in the distance rolling against a blue sky for an incalculable degree of miles. "*Majestic is defined from such a place*," she thought.

Whether it was the emotions of viewing the scenery, the enormity of the realizations accompanying it, the physical exhaustion, or a combination of it all, within a quarter mile, she hit the wall her mentor predicted was inevitable.

Breathing began to become increasingly labored despite the fact she was headed downhill or she had beaten the six-mile mark numerous times before. Panic began to seethe out in awareness that she couldn't go back or forward without having another six miles ahead to trek. Checking the list in her whirling thoughts, she could not find a back door or an easy way out, and she couldn't quit. No one could drive in to pick her up, no one would carry her out, and no one except her mentor knew she needed help.

The mentor saw it before she was able to admit it was there. Kindly, gently the mentor talked to her about taking the next step, dosing her with salt and fuel to gain balance in her electrolytes, and walking by her side, in step with every stride. She began to cry simple tears at first. Then complex ones followed. She trusted the mentor. They had spent months walking together, talking about all the surface things one chat about as miles are charted. From the most bewildering places of her soul, much of the heartache came tumbling out in the stories, explaining why the marathon would be such an important part of her journey and why she had to make it beyond the finish line. The purpose was not simply to say she had completed a marathon, but to prove to herself she could accomplish something beyond the harshness of heavy dominos. More than anything, she needed to take a win.

The details in her stories seemed to startle the mentor, who had no idea why or how she'd gotten to the place at the hilltop. Her girlfriend did. And on a very real level, she transferred the love for her to the mentor. Together they walked five miles before she finished. The last mile was spent in silence as she carried shame for having been so vulnerable. It was not like her.

When they arrived at the check-in point, her girlfriend was waiting. She explained about hitting the wall, being emotional and truly embarrassed, and wanting to go home without coffee. Her girlfriend understood. Before they left, she tried to thank her mentor for sticking with her but felt a difference, distance, and an overly polite demeanor replacing the kindness she misunderstood. They never spoke about it again.

San Francisco came far sooner than she felt ready. The evening before the marathon, the group of racers gathered to decorate running jerseys. She hadn't given it a moment's thought. Feeling quite inadequate and uncreative with glitter or slogans, she wrestled with putting something meaningful on her shirt. Going to scripture, "We walk by faith not by sight," sounded catchy and appropriate. She crafted the identifying verse, 2 Corinthians 5:7 (NKJV) above where her marathon number would go. She called it a day and got a good night's rest.

The next morning was chocked full of electrifying adrenaline as over forty-three hundred marathoners descended on downtown streets. Elbow to shoulder with music blaring from a stage nearly a half-mile in the distance, apartment dwellers from above the street level turned on lights and opened windows to cheer for the marathoners. The festive energy was turned up higher than she could have imagined.

After a big hug, she parted ways with her girlfriend as they traveled different directions. She shuffled through the crowds with her mentor as the anticipation grew toward the starting line. It took nearly an hour to finally cross under the banner strung from one side of the street to the other. They were off to do what they had come to do. Finish.

The weather was cold, damp, and rainy with a heavy fog as they left the downtown. She looked forward to seeing the scenery around the Golden Gate Bridge described by other runners as they trained. It was her first visit to San Francisco, and despite the setbacks she might have faced, she was ready to make this a great day. She was thrilled to be there, confident of her training, and primed to make history in her own personal story. It was October 20, 2013.

Three miles in, her mentor suggested they stop for a restroom break before the port-a-potties turned into disgusting reasons not to use them. When she finished, coming out to where they were to meet, she could see in the distance her mentor had gone ahead. She tried to motion to get her attention, but the mentor ignored the attempt. She felt hurt, angry, and fearful all in the same wave as her hand fell back down by her side.

The next two and a half miles proved to be similar to training with a steady incline up a steep hill with no relief. Each step was bogged down with turmoil as she tried to calm the uncertainty. She had no idea if she were going to hit another wall in the midst of a crowd of strangers. She didn't know what to do once she crossed the finish line, how she was going to get back to her hotel, or even if she would finish. Who would she share her victory with, if she did cross? Or why did the mentor leave her behind? The immense sense of regret weighed heavily on her spirit. She had no idea why she was there or bothered to try. The fog was as thick as her sinking spirit. The beautiful view of the bay, purportedly just to her right, was invisible against the white shield of hazy fog. Visibility was literally only a few yards.

With each heavy step, her face was numb from holding back the tears she had not wakened with early in the morning. Yet each foot remembered the pattern she'd trained in its cadence. Her arms pumped at her waist, and she stood tall against the pull of the hill. From time to time she dropped her head in disbelief. At the top of an enormous hill, a memorial was fashioned with white poster board signs staked in the ground with dedications to those who had lost the battle against deadly diseases. Intended to be inspirational, with the thick fog, it resembled a haunted cemetery. The sight of it rattled her core.

Praying was the only place she had left to go. *"Please, dear God, show me why I am here. This makes no sense to me. I have so much further to go with so many fears. Vulnerabilities only You understand. Somehow, above all else, I know You are here. Please don't leave me here alone."* It was an immature prayer full of self-pity and groaning with the haunting of the past. It was the best she could do.

A small voice next to her asked, "What does the verse on your shirt mean?"

Walking beside her, a woman with short blonde hair and glasses stood about five-foot-three inches tall. She was in runner's gear and wore the number 257 on her jersey. Together they pumped their arms in tempo with each other to join the established pace.

"It is 2 Corinthians 5:7 (NKJV), 'We walk by faith not by sight,'" she replied.

"That is pretty ironic considering the fog, don't you think?" asked the woman.

"No kidding. If you only knew!" The woman's words had struck a deep chord.

"Trust me. I know better than you think." Sadly the woman sounded halfhearted about her conviction.

Yet she was intriguing. "Why? What's your story?"

This unmistakably kind and sentimental woman told her the remarkable story of her husband's death just a couple months earlier from leukemia. They had been best friends for over thirty-five years of life, living and breathing everything it had to offer in the best and worst of times. He alone was her hero. The woman entered the race at the last minute, traveling from Canada to run it by herself to honor him.

She asked the woman if she minded telling her more about him. The next five miles, the woman shared every detail she could recall. They met in high school, but she didn't like him at first. Her mother convinced her to give him a second chance. While their courtship wasn't a whirlwind, it was steady and sturdy in ways where, in her mind, love counts most. They had three grown daughters who were now mothers of sons. He was stern in a quirky way that always left room for a joke or two. Television was one of the things he despised, and ice cream was one of the things he adored. Chocolate was his favorite, but he considered it a sign of integrity to accept any flavor regardless of where it came from.

She talked of how he was a teacher and coach of a girl's volleyball team at the high school. His team went to finals many times and sometimes won championships. Davy, as she called him, had a way of inspiring young adults to find the very best in their dreams and to live them one step at a time, never forgetting the season of preparation meant more than any victory or defeat. His message to the world was simple, uncomplicated, and yet full of life's truths. He was a good man in everything he did and seemingly unremarkable by the world's standards.

She loved him deeply. He didn't know he was sick right away, and because of the health care system in Canada, he wasn't able to get the medical treatment to prolong his life. She wasn't sure he really would have wanted to. They had time to prepare for his death without losing his sense of humor. Above everything, she was pleased to have been by his side to the end.

Now at a loss for what to do with herself, she ran. It gave the woman clarity with the determination she needed. Participating in this race had been a fluke chance. The woman then refocused asking her "Why did you choose that verse for your shirt?"

She had to admit, "I didn't really give it much thought. It seemed catchy last night when everyone was decorating shirts. Now it seems almost prophetic." As the race was unfolding, it meant more to her then when she chose it. It truly felt as the words came by way of a message from the fingertips of a mighty, powerful, and unfathomable hand of God. They were no longer for her alone, but instead a gift for both of them to know He was with them too, even when they couldn't see the Golden Gate Bridge, the future in front of them, or where they were going today.

As unexpectedly as the woman's first question about the writing on her shirt, came the words she blurted out, "Well, I came to run, not walk. Thank you!" And off she ran.

"Wait! I don't know your name," she cried out, yet it didn't deter the woman in the slightest.

Within seconds she was invisible within the fog. Her first reaction was to run after the woman, but she knew she wouldn't be able to catch up. Much of the woman's story held words she needed to hear and put into perspective for her own life. Over the remaining race, she walked through a contemplative prayer in dialogue with God, feeling safe, comforted, and peaceful in a fog of uncertainty. Had anyone been walking with her when the woman came upon reading the verse on her shirt, she doubted the woman would have asked about it. Had the woman not asked about it, she doubted she would have connected it to her own journey in a meaningful way. Without the fog, both of them would have had other things to be in awe of instead of God's hand in their lives for such a time as this. They would have missed each other and indeed perhaps a part of their selves also.

She finished the race with arms in the air. Victory! It made for a great photo, and still she didn't buy a copy of it. Her registered time was respectable but easily forgettable as well. The fog had finally lifted. About fifty feet from the finish line, sections of tables and tents set up a pathway to gather food, aluminum warming blankets, trophies, and medals. Even more tents housed opportunities to buy souvenirs and have a picture taken again. It was a carnival beyond those fifty feet. She wasn't ready to join it. Checking the digital roster posted above the finish line banner, she learned her girlfriend had not come across yet. So she lingered by the temporary fencing, waiting to share her victory.

It fascinated her to watch as others crossed. Any myths she had about what a marathoner may look like quickly vanished. They were short or tall and thin or heavy. Under the myriad of baseball caps were every shade of long or short hair. They were every race, color, and creed. Some were exuberant; others were delirious. Some limped from injuries, and teammates even carried a few. Many raised hands in the air as she had. And just as many couldn't muster the gesture. It had been a journey for all of them, a journey as unique as any one of them were. She thanked God but not in a mighty way. It came with a humble awe of how intricately He had woven this day, even for those who didn't know He had or weren't quite sure anymore.

She looked down at her shoes and scuffed one of them against the ground, a sign of honor for being steadfast through it all. The first tear of the day finally dropped, slowly and within the fog of joy. It was a great day!

As she looked back at those coming across the finish line, she saw a familiar face. The woman she had shared those magical five miles with had her arms in the air, pumping them with every ounce of power left.

"Davy, this one is for you!" she shouted.

Furiously she ran with arms reaching out to grab the woman with everything she had left. "It's you! It's you! I can't believe it's you!"

They collided into an enormous hug, swayed back and forth as they clung to each other, rattling incomprehensible words of celebration. It was a spectacle. In due course they stopped long enough to exchange names, emails, and a vague promise to stay in touch. The woman wanted to get through the tents and back to her room to call her daughters. She wanted to wait for her girlfriend.

With another hug, the woman continued on her journey. She waved good-bye to Davy's wife, and the woman left her standing by the finish line, forever blessed for having walked by faith and not by sight.

Chapter 12: The Illiterate Woman

For everyone who asks receives;
the one who seeks finds;
and to the one who knocks,
the door will be opened.

Luke 11:10

Curiously she watched as the young woman shuffled color-coded index cards, searching for the one believed capable of answering the question. Accentuating the intensity of her wrinkled forehead was the shifting of the young woman's eyes from the cards to her and then back again. At first she was troubled by what the young woman was doing, not because it was necessarily upsetting but because she wasn't sure how to help her. She was convinced, if there were a rock to crawl under, the young would have certainly been there. Instead she shuffled the cards.

In guessing the young woman's age near to thirty, she hesitated because the innocence she portrayed belied the estimation of years. Her long, straight, dishwater blonde hair was far too thin and her eyes blinked with a hint of cheap mascara. A bulky black sweater was intended to mask the brittleness of her body. The young woman was agitated, and as of yet, nothing unexpected during an appointment at a law office warranted it. The attention of the business manager was drawn to the front desk when the young woman refused the receptionist's request to fill out the intake sheet. As the clipboard holding the white sheet of paper covered with questions and black lines reserved for answers was handed to the young woman, she intently glanced at it, pushed it back, and told the receptionist she didn't have to fill it out.

Anything odd in the office landed full-square as responsibility for the business manager. Everything had to be handled by someone, and she was the lucky one who would do it. From her adjacent office, she could overhear the exchange between the young woman and receptionist. It was her intention to redirect the situation when she stepped out. As strange as the young woman's behavior seemed, likewise was the unexpected sense the business manager felt. Privacy would be more effective than the voice of authority coaxing the young woman's cooperation.

She invited the young woman to follow to her office. Even though she wasn't the school principal calling in a rowdy student for a detention, the young woman reacted as if she were. Deliberate and defiant, the young woman reiterated exactly what she previously insisted. She didn't have to fill out the form.

"Well, actually yes you do," the business manager explained. "It isn't simply about us gaining information to help assess if we can represent you. Filling out the intake sheet is also intended to establish if you are able to follow instructions. Doing so is key to preparing for possible litigation. It is only a small step today. If you aren't able to fill out the sheet, it is unlikely one of the attorneys will accept your case."

The young woman's defiance was swapped for uneasiness as she pulled the index cards from her purse and began shuffling them. Taking the pen from the top of the clipboard, the young woman wrote her name on the first line. She held the pen much like a toddler would a fork, awkwardly and out of balance for its purpose. Moving the red card to the bottom of the pile and searching out the green one, the young woman wrote the address on the second line. Copying from the yellow card, she wrote a phone number where the city and state should have been. Skipping the date and time, reason for the appointment, and the remaining questions, the young woman handed back the clipboard, asking if it were all right.

Before accepting it back from the young woman, the business manager walked over to shut the door. Returning to the chair behind the desk, she tenderly tapped the young woman's shoulder twice as she passed before taking the clipboard with her other hand. Scanning it, she read the answers as if they were her own.

"Sweetie, do you know how to read?" she asked.

Joining both embarrassment and relief into one stark reply, the young woman admitted, "No, ma'am, I don't. But I can fill out the form if you tell me what it should say."

"How did you get here?" The business manager's head began spinning with notions about what it must have taken for the young woman to actually locate their office.

"I drove."

"But how did you know our address?"

"I didn't know. Someone else drew this map for me."

The young woman showed her an orange card with handwritten lines directing through stop signs and traffic lights, turning corners and into the parking lot across the street. A big red star was drawn on a box, representing the office with smaller boxes depicting windows and doors.

Her heart broke. "What was it you wanted to see an attorney about?"

"I need to get a divorce from my husband."

"Is he the one who made the map for you?" She didn't actually believe the young woman's husband had, but she wanted to draw out information that didn't come from a prepared response. She supposed the young woman needed someone's help, particularly when navigating a divorce that rarely ends up being as simple as people think it will be.

"No, ma'am. It was my neighbor. She told me the attorney here was nice and would take good care of me. My husband is mean to me. He gave me HIV on purpose because he said then the only one I could have sex with would be him. That way I would never leave him."

"Does he do drugs?" She followed the rabbit trail, hoping the young woman would follow.

"Yes, ma'am. So did I." The young woman pushed up the sleeve of her sweater to show the scars from track marks. "They are much better now. I've been clean from a needle for about a year and a half."

"Okay, so tell me what has happened?"

"He was my boss at the pizza shop, and once he found out I couldn't read, he said he would take care of me if I had sex with him. When I got pregnant, we got married. But the baby died. That's when I started getting drunk a lot. One time when I was really wasted, he talked me into shooting up with him. I knew it was wrong, but I didn't care if I was alive or dead. So I did it. I really liked drinking more than doing drugs because they started to scare me. I stopped shooting for a long, long time. But it was okay because he didn't hurt me. Then he got sick, and the doctor told him he had HIV. Because I was his wife, they tested me too. I didn't have it at the beginning."

The business manager nodded toward the young woman, "Go on."

"He became angry and started blaming me because his life didn't turn out right. I tried to stay with him because he needs me more than I need him now. I stopped drinking and went to AA meetings for a year or more because I had to be sober to take care of him. Until one night when he was real sad and bought me a bottle of champagne to celebrate I didn't have AIDS. I was weak and drank it. We had sex for the first time since he found out. After that, I figured I'd get it sooner or later, so we kept doing it. Now he is so mean to me that I don't think I can take care of him anymore."

"Have you been tested again?" There was something unusually compelling in how the young woman didn't believe she had become infected quite yet.

"No, I don't need to. I know he is right."

"Sweetie, what would you like to do?"

It was naïve, but she was searching for an escape for the young woman, one where all the injustices ever done could be redeemed by the mighty, powerful, and unfathomable hand of God. They only needed to find the first step and take a leap of faith.

"I wish I could be normal. But I'm not smart enough for normal because I can't read." The young woman looked down at the colored index cards held in her right hand. They held a full deck of shame.

As it spilled from her eye, a tear dropped onto the orange card, became absorbed, and marked the spot with a darker shade. Defeat bore down, imitating wild cattle stampeding with the force of relentless drive over innocence, leaving nothing in the path unharmed. She both pitied and loved the young woman.

Even so, she turned away to regain her composure. Looking out the window, she saw a large butterfly resting on the outside of the pane of glass. It was the most vibrant blue, unmatched only by the color of the brightest sky. Circling the rim of its wings was a dark brown, nearly black band seeming to outline and protect the blue from falling into midair. As the leaves rustled on the nearby tree, it held tight to its place with a fragile dignity only something of beautiful determination can know intimately. It was captivating.

"Do you have a blue card?" She focused back and detected the butterfly caught the young woman's attention too.

"Yes, I do. Somewhere in here."

She scrounged through her purse until finding a blue card, vacant from any writing or maps. Reaching across the desk to hand it to her, the young woman recognized the air in the room had shifted from pity to hope. Yet she didn't realize with it so had her life.

On one side of the card, the business manager began to sketch one of the feeblest renditions of a butterfly anyone might imagine. She outlined the wings with a marker from her desk, portraying it as closely as she was able to the one visiting on the other side of the glass.

Flipping over the card, she scribbled in bold letters, "I am smart."

"My sweet friend, I want you to listen to me carefully. Anyone who can drive to our office by following the map you have is smart. Anyone who can memorize which cards should be copied into which lines is smart. Anyone who can stop drinking and doing drugs is smart. And certainly anyone who can take care of a sick husband is smart. I want you to read the back of this card for me. What do you think it says?"

Hesitating, the young woman guessed, "I am smart?" She was indeed bright enough to read.

"Yes! It does! And this is what I want you to know. There is simply no reason for a butterfly to be on the outside of the window any more then there is a reason why you should be sitting here right now. It is just as simple as why you don't know how to read. No matter the reason, you weren't given the opportunity others were to learn. But just like the butterfly, there is no reason why you can't learn to read if you're given a chance. If I can find someone to teach you, do you want to learn?"

"Do you think I can?"

"Think? Sweetie, I know you can! I am convinced, if you want to learn, it will happen. I have friends who can help you. What do you think?" Just as she asked, movement caught their attention as they both looked toward the window where the butterfly did what it came to do, to fly.

It took a couple days and several phone calls before she was able to get everything arranged. In the meantime the young woman moved in with the neighbor who drew maps and helped manage her index cards. Her husband was angry. Yet he was not as angry as the young woman was hopeful. When the business manager called to give the directions and contact information to get started, the young woman told her it would be written on the blue card beneath the butterfly drawing.

It was almost a year later when the business manager heard the young woman's voice again at the front desk.

"I'd like to fill out an intake sheet please," she informed the new girl sitting there.

"Do you have an appointment?" the receptionist asked.

"Go ahead. Let her fill one out," the business manager said, again coming from her office to override the policy one more time.

There was no appointment and no longer any need for a divorce. But there was a whole lot of reason to fill out the intake sheet. When the young woman finished, she was invited into the principal's office again. Only this time it was as an honor student coming to share her gratitude and tell a story of an adventure in becoming normal.

Chapter 13: The Closet Man

Therefore I tell you,
do not worry about your life,
what you will eat or drink;
or about your body, what you will wear.
Is not life more than food,
and the body more than clothes?

Matthew 6:25

When wire shelving holding clothing breaks out of the wall, crashing on the floor of the closet, there is a defining sound screaming of disaster. In the middle of the night, it is, in fact, much louder. She knew because it wasn't the first time the rack tumbled into a pile of hangers wrinkling her fashion choices.

Her landlord repaired it the first time. Enduring a lecture on spending too much money on clothing was the cost for his help. It took less time for him to repair the rack then it did for her to move the clothing from the closet floor to the extra bedroom to make room for his help. Keeping her thoughts to herself, she was skeptical about how securely he was able to fix it. Wholeheartedly she hoped he knew what he was doing.

He proved her skepticism was well-placed. A few weeks later, days after her rent had been raised, the clothing rack fell again. Calling her landlord held very little appeal. She reconciled herself to using the extra bedroom as a wardrobe storeroom. Many frustrating days of tugging this or that from the bottom of a pile prompted her to use it as an excuse for being late on a dinner date with a potential suitor. As heartfelt as she intended her explanation to be, it sounded closer to whining, even to her. Living in the South translates a woman whining into a call to chivalry for most self-respecting gentlemen. His response to offer help surprised her, for as a natural-born Northerner, she hardly considered it a possibility. Nevertheless she watched in gratitude while he reinforced the toggle bolts, assuring her it wouldn't happen again as fault clearly lie with whoever installed it previously.

Fortunately or unfortunately, depending on one's perspective, the closet remained intact long after she stopped dating him . . . until the third charming time when it came crashing down in the middle of the night. Without a man in her life and even less regard for her landlord, it seemed she was on her own to face the new challenge. All the anthems, slogans, or clichés in the world couldn't protect her from her own little pity party. She felt like a helpless idiot. Yet somehow it was also a clear reminder to try.

First she convinced herself the wire shelving was junk. If two different men couldn't get it right, perhaps another game plan was in order.

"How tough could it be to try the old-fashioned way with a rod and brackets? I'm smart enough to figure this out," she told herself.

If she were careful and took her time, she was convinced she could actually succeed at refurbishing her closet. Her mother, on the other hand, found the idea rather funny as they chatted on the phone while she drove to the hardware store. Suggesting she wander around, batting her eyes, playing the damsel in distress act until a Southern gentleman felt sorry enough to help was how her mother encouraged her. The other two closet disasters had not been included when she explained the predicament to her mother. It seemed reasonable, if she were going to avoid a lecture from the landlord, she should consider avoiding one from her mother as well. Besides she really wanted to do this her own way, a notion missing from their mother-daughter dance.

After defending her position, her mother mockingly asked where was God when she needed help. They didn't see eye to eye on faith either. She believed, and her mother questioned. Her mother's words struck a vulnerable spot. With them came all the reasons why she should run until she reached the end of the earth and then jump off. Run from all the places where she didn't feel sure of herself, run from a history of disappointment in those who were no longer here to help and run from the judgment of others whose words tore down instead of built her up. And finally to run from all the unexplainable disasters.

"*Simply run*," she thought

She wasn't ready to hang the brackets or rod, and she knew it. There were no more clichés playing in her head, instead simply a problem she had to have faith she could work through if she tried. She prayerfully laid it in the mighty, powerful, and unfathomable hands of God, but not because it was a big earth-shattering problem calling for the attention of the Master of the Universe. Instead because, wrapped in all her vulnerabilities, the closet was an everyday trial coming from the act of picking up her cross. The very same cross that is rarely about what one might think it is but rather grown from the same wood created by the Father into a magnificent tree for shade and rest.

The lights seemed brighter than usual as she walked into the hardware store. Even the concrete floors were hard under her steps, while the sounds echoed in aisles empty of onlookers. It was a hollow place decorated from floor to ceiling with the useful things of repair. In aisle 12B, the shelves of shelves displayed far more options than she wanted to consider. Even so, she walked to both ends three or maybe four times to reinforce the idea of old-fashioned rods and brackets. Indeed they seemed the simplest.

Trying to discern which one to use, she held a white triangle rod support in her left hand, examining how it would attach to the wall. For the most part, it made sense, except for one set of holes she couldn't figure out. Picking a similar one to compare, she noticed someone walking down the aisle toward her.

Partially looking up, she saw a man perhaps in his early thirties approaching. He was tall and athletically thin with broad shoulders where his scraggly blonde hair skirted the edge of a collar to a long-sleeved, white T-shirt pushed up at the elbow. The denim trousers and work boots completed a contractor's uniform. His face was chiseled with ruggedness, and his brown eyes were clear with purpose.

Trying to return her focus on the two brackets, she couldn't help being distracted by his jostling of silver metal rods positioned to lean upright in the bin next to where she stood. He took one from the bin to examine it more closely, returned it, tried another, and then another and so on. He was cautious to keep the ones he rejected separate from the others to be examined until his efforts became futile. The rods shifted, falling forward to tumble about both of them. She automatically reached to catch the two outside his reach, sorting the leftovers and repositioning them back safely.

"Thanks," he said. "I want to find one without any scratches."

"Won't the hangers leave scratches?" she asked, a bit baffled by his logic.

"Sure, but not until someone hangs them on the rod. I'm a closet contractor for new construction of custom homes. They need to be perfect when the owner inspects the closet. After that, I could care less."

The conversation with her mother came sailing back in full force as she looked back at the brackets in her hands. She did not want to be a damsel in distress, bat her eyelashes, or appear helpless. Nonetheless they were in the same aisle in a virtually empty store. He was an expert, and she could use some advice.

Awkwardly she took the chance. "Hey, do you know what these extra holes are for?"

"What are you trying to do?" he ignored her question, turning his attention away from the metal rods.

She explained how the wire racks had fallen, and she planned to replace them with brackets and rods.

He laughed. "If the wire racks were fastened into a stud, they wouldn't come down. You do know what a stud is, don't you?" he asked teasingly.

"Of course I do. So does the guy who fixed it last time when it fell. As a matter of fact, my landlord does too. I watched him fasten it to studs when it came down the time before that. So I think it is time for a change. Don't you agree?" He was beginning to irritate her, and she half-regretted asking his advice.

"Actually no, I wouldn't agree. If those wire racks were installed properly, nothing should make them come out of the wall. I don't care how many clothes you have hanging on it. They are rated to hold a hundred and fifty pounds per foot, and unless you're hanging concrete, they should be fine. I can show you. Come over here."

He led her to the section where the wire racks were displayed. On the label it clearly indicated what he said was true.

"I don't know what to tell you. All I know is they keep falling off, and I have to figure something out."

"Why don't you ask the guy who fixed it last time?"

"That sounds easy enough, except we aren't dating anymore so I doubt if he'd be real keen about repairing something he thinks he already fixed. Besides I don't want to give him the impression it's an invitation to have dinner."

Reaching into his pocket, he pulled out a business card and handed it to her. "I'll tell you what. Give me a call, and

I'll find some time to slide you in my schedule and take a look at it in between jobs tomorrow. I just need your number on my phone to call when I'm headed your direction. Text me your address."

"Thanks, but I really can't afford to hire someone to do a job I can do myself."

"Don't worry about that. I'm just going to take a look at it. You can trust me. I'm harmless." Then he grabbed one of the metal rods and walked away with a toss of his hand in the air as he rounded the corner at the end of the aisle.

All the reasons why she shouldn't call him bombarded her as a landslide of irrational logic might. Still she trusted something about him. Sending the information he asked for, she put the triangle back on the shelf and left the hardware store. On a very real level, she wasn't convinced he would respond.

About ten thirty the next morning, the call came, saying he would stop by around noon. True to his word, he pulled up to her house in a big, shiny, white pickup truck with a construction logo matching his business card on the side panel. She led him through her bedroom and the adjacent bathroom into the closet.

After inspecting the walls, he looked closer at the shelving lying on the floor. "Here's your problem," he said, pointing to the clasp for the bracket. "You were right. They were installed into the studs. But they weren't leveled. When just one clasp is out of alignment, it pulls on the other ones. Look, they are flimsy plastic so, with enough pressure, one breaks, and the others follow like a domino effect. Really all you need are some metal clasps and one new bracket because this one is bent. It should cost less than ten dollars. The other materials will be fine to reuse."

"Are you sure?" she asked, a little dismayed at how simple he made it sound.

"Yes. Can you paint?" he asked.

"Ahhh ya, I suppose. Why?"

"I think, if we patch and repaint the wall, your landlord will never know. It will be better than new. What do you think?"

"How much will it cost for you to do it?"

"I noticed you have a Kairos name badge on the counter in your bathroom. Do you go?"

Kairos was the name of a worship service on Tuesday evenings designed for young adults at her church.

"Yes. Actually I serve as a counselor. I'm fairly involved at church."

"No kidding? I guess that's why you have a pile of badges?"

Looking back over her shoulder to the badges laying in the middle of her counter in between the two sinks, she said, "Yes, they like me to wear a different badge for each ministry. You could say I'm all over the place. Do you go? How do you know about Kairos?"

"I used to go when I was younger. Not really in church these days. I'm trying to sort out some stuff. I'll tell you what. I can come back tomorrow to spackle and fill the damage to the wall if you'll paint it when I'm finished. Then I'll install this stuff back to normal. Don't worry about the cost because I won't charge you. Consider it my good deed for the week."

"Wow! That sounds great. Thanks! Sure I'll paint the wall, but are you sure?"

"Don't think anything of it. I'll call when I'm on my way."

The next day he was in her closet less than ten minutes spackling and filling the holes in the wall. After a second day of sanding, he left marching orders for her to get the wall painted. It struck her he was a take-charge, no-nonsense sort of guy with an acute sense of value for his time, something he didn't waste with conversation. She didn't know anything about him apart from being a stranger who stepped off the beaten path to help her. And she appreciated it more than she guessed he would probably ever know.

Merely saying "thank you" sounded hollow in comparison to how she valued his help. It wasn't simply about the closet or clothing in the spare bedroom. Fixing her closet was about being the benefactor of an unexpected act of goodwill with no strings attached. Many times she believed kindness was viewed as the initiation of negotiations where the recipient is left with an unspoken bill of expectation. And for those who become comfortable giving apart from reciprocity, a quietness often speaks louder then the act itself. Sadly kindness may hold an additional weight, knowing you may be taken for granted or, worse, taken advantage of. Quietness is the acceptance of both and more.

He worked diligently in much the same way. It was within his character to serve for the sheer purity of doing so without thought of balancing the scale. It would have been easier for him to install the wire rack without giving a second thought for the wall. There is nothing slipshod about kindness. It moves in the realm of excellence while rebuffing anything less.

The day he was to finish the project, she cooked a batch of spaghetti sauce and pasta with a sideline of her favorite Italian salad and bread for him. She was a cook, and if you know anything about cooks, you know cooks cook. It is one of the finer small miracles in life, to create something nurturing for someone while it in turn nurtures you. Part of her *modus operandi* was to prepare far more than a single meal. The spaghetti was no exception as she packed every bit of it into the extra large containers.

Despite enjoying the preparation, as time grew closer for him to return, she felt anxiousness creeping in, which next turned into second-guessing herself about if preparing food for him would appear weird, corny, or whatever. She didn't know if a wife or girlfriend of his would question where the meal came from, if he liked spaghetti, or if it would be awkward. He had so very casually tossed her his card without a hesitation, while she, on the other hand, toiled about the gesture.

He arrived precisely as expected to finish installing the wire rack while she watched. At one point he nonchalantly asked her to hold one end of the rack while he leveled the brackets. Her assistance was no big deal for him. Yet it truly reinforced for her that she was contributing and not a damsel totally in distress. Once they were close to finishing, she quietly mentioned fixing the meal. With her gesture to offer food, his façade cracked wide open. He was hungry.

Perhaps it would have been fine if it were one of those it's-time-to-eat hungry moods. But it wasn't. He hadn't had a meal in three days and was living in his truck. The story unfolded quickly as he hit the important facts, leaving out many details. He owned a home building company that had failed a few months earlier.

The night after closing on the sale of a house, a fire destroyed it. There was an investigation of arson, prompting the insurance company to deliberately not pay on the claim for months. The family who bought the house from him had their life in boxes on a moving van with nowhere to land. Facing a tough choice to leave the burden where he legally could, with the new owners, he chose a different option. Instead he offered the buyers another home down the same street that cost him twenty-five thousand dollars more to build. He refused the advice of his attorney to pass the difference on to the new owners. The gesture caused him to fall behind on the contractor's loans as he waited on the insurance company. Time wasn't on his side. The dominos started to fall, and with them, his company, reputation, home, and, ultimately, his church family.

He explained how he was trying to start over now by taking meager jobs that others wouldn't find profitable. Closets were easy, and business cards were cheap.

"If I can build a house, with the help of God, I should be able to rebuild my life," he said with the sincerity of a person who categorically lived the cliché he wrote for himself.

The client who hired him to install the closet when they met at the hardware store, cut his proceeds in half after finding scratches on the rod he installed. The money meant nothing beyond a negotiation to them. To him, it was what he depended on for food since his truck payment took the rest.

Seeing tears well up in her eyes caused his to become watery too. "Before coming in here today, I sat in my truck in your driveway, praying God would provide manna for me. I love God, but there are some days I really dislike the world He created."

They finished hanging the wire shelving in silence. As he was leaving, she asked, "Is there anything else I can do to help? We can have dinner together or perhaps I have a few dollars in my purse."

"No thank, you. That won't be necessary. I won't need anything else. The food is what I prayed for. This is enough to hold me over for a few more days. I expect God will show up then too. But you're kind to offer. Thank you again."

She tried to call him three or four times. He didn't answer, and she wondered if his phone service were shut off until she received a text message from him saying, "Some trust in chariots and some in horses, but we trust in the name of the Lord our God. I'm fine."

Chapter 14: The Graveside Son

Your relatives, members of your own family—
even they have betrayed you;
they have raised a loud cry against you.
Do not trust them,
though they speak well of you.

Jeremiah 12:6

Sitting next to her on the passenger seat of her car, a small bouquet of colorful flowers in a yellow vase sustained her resolve to find a proper place to deliver them. They were ordinary spring blooms, arranged tightly in the shape of a rounded, upside-down bowl. The clear plastic cardholder stuck in the center displayed a small envelope with "Happy Mother's Day" printed on the front. She did not open it to read the enclosed card. The bouquet had come as expected, delivered by a stranger ringing her doorbell in the middle of the afternoon on the second Sunday in May.

In previous years she had either waited for the flowers to age gracefully or unceremoniously deposited them in the garbage within minutes of arrival. It had only been the first two years when receiving the flowers provided a fleeting sense of joy and a spark of hope. Now they were a deadly reminder she had been dismissed by the obligatory and ever-so-casual order placed with a florist.

Raindrops on her windshield became blurry as she looked out over the cemetery. While she contemplated her next step, a heavy mist replaced the afternoon showers, and time passed slower than she predicted. The evenly manicured grass beamed like green polish, uniting each blade into a blanket of protection for the graves. Scattered about in even rows, hardly negligible in their dissimilarity, headstones commingled into conformity as the lives beneath them hadn't. Trees and flowering shrubs were arranged along the pathways to mimic a natural setting, when instead they were meticulously planned, planted, and pruned specifically to adapt to the unnatural.

It has been readily accepted the worst thing a mother could ever experience is burying her own child. Sadly the sentiment is wrapped around a child who died, not one who lived. And the burying is actually done by a stranger. Someone else will put the child in a box, dig a hole, lower the box into it, begin to shovel dirt on top, place the marker, and walk away. It was grief heavier than anyone should bear.

"*If that is the worst*," she thought, "*what is it when your own child causes you to place your feelings of love into a box, dig a hole, lower the box into it, shovel the dirt, mark it, and walk away, knowing they are alive? Every day. Every moment.*"

The continuous burial process ultimately is absorbed into the endless brigade of memories or reminders, social settings, and holidays. It is there in quiet moments and in the heartsick feelings that refuse to fade. The gravesite is endlessly re-created, only with one remarkable difference. The mother left aside tends to the ritual caretaking by shutting the box, digging the hole, lowering the box into it, shoveling the dirt, marking it, and walking away.

She had not lost her children to a dreadful accident or horrific illness. But instead they were lost to an avoidably insidious betrayal from their callously hardened hearts and the rejection of obligatory silence. No words were spoken, not a single one given in consideration for a hint of reconciliation, creating a void where an explanation loitered in silence. She was merely required to move on, bury her motherhood, and live at the gravesite. The piercing dismissiveness of judgment and speculation from others took the place where comfort would have been offered, if instead they had died. And in those deeply held moments with God, she wasn't granted a place to rest her children with Him in heaven.

No one should have to bear reliving the moments at a gravesite in silence, alone and with the hostility of mistaken opinions. She had committed no sin to warrant it, nor a mistake justifying it. There simply was no explanation, excuse, or reason worthy of its infliction. None. Not even the trite excuse given to mothers of deceased children, "God needed another angel in heaven."

Her children remained in this ugly world, silent. To replace grief, hope had been the dangling expectation serving as yet another layer of torture no mother should be asked to bear. She had exhausted herself with humiliating attempts to heal the wounds for all of them. After time, the cruelty of it succumbed to the numbness of proxy acceptance until a random avalanche of pain would dump her back into the darkness.

She is a middle-aged woman standing five-foot-six with blue eyes and no tattoos, two children and a half-dozen grandchildren. Her demographic characteristics read without names, personalities, or meaning. To intentionally conceal the appearance of the gravesite, when asked, she shared stories about her children, told far too many times without an update. The anecdotes were old and dreadfully bittersweet, stories only as valuable as a sheet of white paper with properly checked boxes. And she wondered if grief would begin a healing course if she could simply mark the boxes as none.

When asked whether she had youngsters, she smiled politely and said, "It would have been lovely, but no."

What if she erased them from who she was, as they seemingly had erased her?

Then the flowers arrived. Despite all of his hurriedness, the deliveryman recognized this particular bouquet was not received, as other mothers would do. Watching her sign the receipt, he felt uncomfortable with her ignorance of his embarrassment in witnessing what should have been private wounds. Before she shut the door between them, he had already turned away, trusting her grief wouldn't be contagious. And indeed it wasn't. Mother's Day continued as she leaned back on the closed door, holding tightly the bouquet and her breath with it.

"Perhaps if I don't breathe," she thought, *"it won't hurt as much."*

She was wrong. She was well-practiced in efforts she referred to as "the art of ignoring it until she had to get over it." Each time a reminder dropped in place, it was skillfully disregarded as she turned away or shielded herself in the disgraceful denial she wore as protection. The delivery of the flowers meant time was now gesturing menacingly to her duty where she would get over it. She knew it would come. Without fail, it always did.

She dedicated herself to making this time different. After driving through rain to the cemetery, she now watched the leftover drops on the windshield fade. It had to be done. She reached for the bouquet, took the card from the plastic holder, scrunched it in the palm of her hand before putting it in her pocket, grasped the door handle, pulled it open, and stepped from her car. The humidity was nearly as heavy as her spirit. Neither would be a deterrent as she sluggishly paced up and down the rows of headstones, sporadically stopping to read the engravings. She was searching to find one holding some semblance of meaning, where leaving the flowers next to it could prove to be significant, despite being deceptively anonymous for a stranger. She would know.

Then just as God's mighty, powerful, and unfathomable hand often does, she was guided to a grave, four steps over and just to the left. "*It is prettier than many of the others,*" she thought.

The headstone was intricately carved with flowers across the top, a cross with a crown of thorns in the middle, and two doves under the name and dates. The first date was her son's birthday, and the second date was her daughter's. The years revealed he had been gone nearly a decade before her children were born.

Kneeling down, she placed the flowers at the base of the headstone. She supposed her son had sent them, but the card remained crumpled and unread in her pocket. "*The man buried beneath her must have been a Christian,*" she thought, contemplating the engraved crown of thorns. Ever so slowly she reached out to rest her right hand on the top of the gravestone, bowed her head, and began to pray. She was heartbroken.

Her faith had taught her a compassionate, loving, merciful God fully understood, and yet she needed someone close, a very human person to know. Being alone today made her feel the distance between the world and eternity would never provide a bridge she could walk. And the masquerade of accepting her loss would be the biggest deception between her and her heavenly Father. She began to weep.

The weeping worsened into sobs until she laid her head on the cold stone, hugging it for every bit of protection from the collapse she sensed would soon come. Suffering far too long as the caregiver of her children's gravesite, she pleaded for God to take her home. As her shoulders heaved, she felt the weight of a strong, sturdy hand placed on her right arm to calm her.

"*It can't be real,*" she thought until she heard the quiet voice ask her, "What can I do to help?"

Turning, she saw a man kneeling on one knee next to her. He was dressed in a crisp black clergy shirt with a white tab in the front of his collar, coordinating trousers, and shoes.

His short grayish, brown hair nearly matched the concern in his eyes.

"What is upsetting you?" he asked again.

"I'm sorry. I'll be all right. I'm just having a tough day, and well ..." She trailed off as she glanced down at the flowers.

"He was my grandfather, my mother's father. Did you know him?" he asked.

"Ummmm, no. I'm sorry I didn't mean to disturb you. I should go." She began to stand, balancing herself against the stone as she brushed the wet dirt and grass from her pant legs.

He followed her lead to rise. "But your flowers. Did you want to take them with you?"

Awkwardly she refused, "No, no. You can have them. It's all right. I don't need them." Entwined in her sorrow, was now a thick dose of embarrassed.

"Can I tell you a story about my grandfather before you go?"

"I guess, I mean I don't know ... I suppose." She wanted to run, get lost between the other headstones, lose track of where she was, and never return.

"As cliché as this may sound, he was one of the finest men I've ever known. You would have liked him. Everyone did, except me for a while there. You see, I went through a period of time when I was stupidly distant from my mother. I'm not sure what caused it apart from I was just a hard-hearted fool. While her heart broke, I was completely self-absorbed and oblivious. Now my grandfather, it didn't break his heart as much as it made him angry. He tracked me down several times, confronting me man-to-man. My dad wasn't in the picture at the time, and I guess, if anyone had a right to call me out, he did. You know, I still didn't get it until the day he died. At his funeral I saw my mother for the first time. Before that, she was just someone who I ran from. I figured out that day, it was truly myself I was running from. All she did was love me well, in spite of myself. I didn't deserve it. Not one bit. But she never gave up on me, brokenhearted and all." He pointed to the grave just to the right of where they stood. "She danced into heaven on Mother's Day last year. Now I know what a broken heart truly feels like."

Tears welled up in her eyes, streaking down her face, "Ya, I know what it truly feels like too." She trembled. "My kids ..." She couldn't finish her sentence, and for him, she didn't need to. Fumbling with her hand in her pocket, she felt the crumpled-up envelope that still wasn't opened. Pulling it out, she handed it to him with her shaking hand. "I should go."

She turned and headed back to the car with the rain-drops on the windshield. He stood watching as she pulled out and left the cemetery. Uncurling the paper she handed him, he opened the envelope and read the logo of the florist and the typed inscription of her son's name.

"It wouldn't be tough to track him down," he thought.

Even if her son didn't want to hear what he had to say, man-to-man, he owed it to both their mothers to try.

Chapter 15: The Traveling Jeweler

Do not give dogs what is sacred;
do not throw your pearls to pigs.
If you do, they may trample them under their feet,
and turn and tear you to pieces.

Matthew 7:6

The rows and rows of diamond rings dazzled even the most discerning eye; still he was hardly as seasoned as the price tags suggested one ought to be. He wondered how a groom-to-be became experienced in buying an engagement ring when simply parking the car a few steps beyond the doorway was unsettling. The portico sheltered oversized Gothic pillars adorned by the watchful yet menacing eyes of dual lion statues perched above head height, positioned as greeters onto the red carpet and beckoning toward the massive wrought iron entrance.

The doors did not swing open until after the small golden buzzer positioned to the right alerted an anonymous gatekeeper, who acknowledged confirmation of an appointment through a matching intercom box. Unmistakable was the buzzer sounding just seconds before the thunk of the door and then again locking behind him as he stepped in.

A man dressed in a severely black suit and donning a prominently plastic smile fastened precisely on his face, held out his hand for an introduction then guided him to the right toward a seat in front of an oversized mahogany desk. The room was lined with vignettes of glass showcases each flaunting gems flashing under the impeccably fastidious lighting. In the center a chandelier of crystals dangled from a ceiling coated with countless layers of hues in gold and silver swirls. Massive bouquets of vividly arranged flowers in tall vases were scattered about in even formation balanced against the ornate golden mirrors masquerading as a barrier for secret witnesses. From beyond the inside of his chest, the punching of his heart pounded with greater intensity than the rhythm of unheard background music specifically piped in to soothe the anxiety of unfamiliar quiet. The interrogation began.

It was the first time his seven years of college, four major professional promotions, and a nest egg his parent couldn't begin to imagine, seemed meager in comparison to expectations. Under normal circumstances, he would have excused himself from any situation that demoralized his veracity as this one did. He had not been born or raised with a silver spoon. Nor would he willingly choose to be judged as someone who had. Any accomplishments he claimed as his own had been earned through the demanding work of every day. Still this is where her persistent cues pointed each time he skirted around the subject of a proposal.

His soon to be fiancé was beautiful - tall, athletic, with long, dark hair and brown eyes big enough to fall into. She was also smart, well-educated, accomplished, and, by any standards, the perfect woman. They met a year earlier backstage at a charitable fund-raiser where both were being auctioned for a date in exchange for hefty donations. Together they laughed about the awkwardness, saying it was for a good cause.

To his astonishment, she happily accepted the invitation to parlay it into a double date with their prospective winners. Bids for her were considerably higher than those for him, making him feel as if it were indeed he who had actually won the auction. The date itself quickly turned into a shared camaraderie, kicking off a romance neither expected.

"It is time," he thought.

Time to make the proverbial commitment to wife and home, and to begin a future with someone. His friends had all taken the plunge. His parents often encouraged him to give it consideration. And as a man, the idea of leaving the superficial world of dating possessed significant appeal. All he needed was the perfect bride, and that she was.

After being awkwardly yet duly qualified by the plastic smiling, black suited man he then listened to the recitation of clarifications on the intricacies of buying a diamond. With it were the subtle pressure techniques reserved for a once-in-a-lifetime decision. Outwardly he posed politely. However inwardly he felt meaningfully dismissiveness of the man's recommendation. He had already spent numerous hours researching the many options that had then shaped his budget. With the conventional guidelines of spending three times a monthly income, his purchase would be beyond the highest annual salary of his father's lifetime. With or without the sanctions of the plastic smile, he intended to select the engagement ring on his own terms. It started to occur to him the process might be more complicated then he originally anticipated.

The selling dance between him and the plastic smile had gotten off to a rocky start when the first ring suggested was equal in value to double the parameters disclosed during the interrogation. Each successive option was, in his mind, equally inappropriate. He hated the sense of inadequacies being imposed on him. The thumping of his chest ceased as resolution hardened into obvious tension between the two of them. She wanted a ring from this particular jeweler, and he wanted to give it to her. He had a budget in mind and intended to stick to it. It escaped him why this was difficult for the plastic smile to accommodate.

With marginal indifference, he vaguely noticed another man enter through the door behind one of the display cases to the left. The man loitered in the peripheral, waiting patiently for a suitable place to join the conversation.

"I see you haven't found the perfect piece yet," the man said with a thick European accent.

"No, we're still working on it," he replied with noticeable frustration.

The man nodded at the plastic smiling salesman, who then excused himself and disappeared behind the door from where the man had emerged.

"Tell me, sir, what is it you are here to find?" the man gently asked as he looked up at him inquisitively.

The elderly man was short, maybe five-foot-five, and wearing a wrinkled, ill-fitting gray suit draped haphazardly over his frail posture. The wire-rimmed spectacles resting on the end of his nose were bent and out of shape. They seemed to coordinate well with his olive-toned skin and thinning hair combed from one side of his head to the other. Shuffling as he walked, he moved from behind the showcase to the side where they could both view the many rings together.

"I'm looking for an engagement ring."

"Aaah yes, an important decision. Would you mind telling me about her? Perhaps it will help to understand what would best fit her style."

"She's beautiful, like a model. It's important to her the ring tells the world how much I care about her."

"And how much do you care about her?" the man asked with an uncanny frankness.

"I care about her a lot." His defensiveness imitated a gong being struck to warn of the rising symbol of determination.

"Aaah, I see." The old man pondered and paused. And then after shuffling a half step closer, he proceeded, "How did you choose this shop?"

"It is the one she suggested. She said this is the best jeweler in the state."

"I can vouch for the fact that they actually are one of the best."

"They? Do you work here?"

"I suppose technically yes, but officially not. I'm an investor who buys and sells gems worldwide."

"I'm surprised the salesman left us alone on the floor together then."

"Don't be. We're both on surveillance, and the doors are locked so neither of us can leave until they accommodate our departure."

"Oh, I see. Or until I buy something more in line with their expectation rather than my own?"

Shifting gears, the man asked, "Would you consider a pearl ring instead of a diamond?"

"No. Why would you ask that? Engagement rings are usually diamonds."

"Not always. Natural pearls are a romantic jewel, the oldest gem, and very rare with significant meaning. Do you know the Hymn of Pearls?"

"No, I don't. But it wouldn't matter. I'm sure my girlfriend is definite about wanting a diamond. Her friends ..." He left the remainder of his thought to trail off unspoken.

"Please, don't take offense, young man, but you hardly seem the type who is governed by status symbols. Something is missing in your description, the intimacy of being truly delighted by her. I've observed plenty of arranged marriages in my lifetime, and yours seems to have many of the earmarks of convenience. Do you love her?"

"I suppose so. Who wouldn't?"

"I dare say if you would listen to the wisdom of an old man." Then he solemnly added, "That isn't enough."

"Are you saying I shouldn't marry her because I won't spend more on a ring? You don't know anything about us."

"No. I'm saying you don't appear to be madly, deeply, and passionately in love with her. Nor she with you, regardless of how much is spent," the old man spoke quietly and gently with the voice of wisdom. "It is easy to find yourself in a position where it makes perfect sense. If getting married is more about how the ring, the wedding, the address, and the name all look to the world, you will forfeit the one extraordinary thing you have to intimately reveal in each other. Tell me something. Do you believe you are God's best for her?"

"I haven't thought about it in those terms before. Who can say who is best for someone else?"

"Men who are the best for their wives know it. Furthermore they will say they are without hesitation or second thoughts. Not out of arrogance, mind you, but rather from knowing she inspires him to be what God intended as the best for both of them."

"I know I care about her. I know we are good together. And I know we would make a good life for each other. Isn't that enough?"

"Perhaps. But would you rather have more than enough?"

"Enough is good enough for me."

"Is it good enough for her?"

"I suppose so."

"Excuse me for a minute, young man. I'll be right back." The short man with glasses shuffled back behind the ominous door where secrets and escapes from uncomfortable conversations were hidden.

Standing there alone, the young man looked in the mirror, wondering exactly who was watching. "*Not that it makes much difference*," he thought.

Turning to face the massive, locked wrought iron doors at the front of the store, he leaned back on the display case, exposing his back to the watchful eyes behind the mirror. With both hands in the pockets of his trousers, his shoulders instinctively rolled forward as he examined the carpet beneath his shoes now crossed at the ankles. The words of the old man began to trouble him. "*Was he trying to fill in the blanks of his life without considering what God's best would be? And what about her? Did he simply fit into an easy equation the world around them would affirm? Did he love her, or did he care for her?"* Question upon question began to topple over one another, each devoid of respite from an answer.

Several minutes passed. Locked in the free-fall of questions, he didn't notice when the old man returned, lingering quietly on the other side of the display case. His own rounded shoulders grew heavier, his throat began to thicken, and his stomach tightened in preparation for a severe blow. The otherwise stillness of his left shoe randomly twitched, showing the only evidence of any contorting happening within him.

"Did you have any questions, young man?" the older gentleman delicately asked.

"Yes, I suppose I do. But I'm not sure they are about rings," he apologetically replied.

"Perhaps today isn't the day for you to find what you were looking for. I've spoken with the salesman, and he told me what you intended to spend. It is quite a respectable amount affording many choices of beautiful rings. I've also opened an account in your name and placed a matching credit equal in value to what you had in mind to be applied toward your selection. It is yours to have, freely and without obligation. However, I would encourage you not to use it until you wholeheartedly believe you are God's best for the woman you will buy a ring for. Do you understand?"

"No, not really. I don't understand. Why would you do such a thing?"

"Unlike my colleague, making a sale today isn't what I'm here to do. You remind me far too much of myself many years ago when I too stood in similar shoes. I made the wrong choice. It ended very badly, becoming one of the deepest regrets of my life. One never completely recovers from such a misstep, even if you do learn to move on. I would encourage you to take some time. Really study scripture, be prayerful, and wait for the mighty, powerful, and unfathomable hand of God to guide you. If you find your girlfriend is part of the plan, you will be better equipped to be God's best for her.

Or you can come back tomorrow and buy a dazzling diamond everyone will be duly impressed with. It's your choice, my boy. Choose wisely."

The old man motioned toward the massive wrought iron doors, shuffled as they walked toward it, and then shook his hand just as the thunk of the lock sounded. The pillars, lions, and red carpet were no longer ominous barriers but rather a fortress defending wisdom.

For the next three years, he fondly recalled the old man each time his path randomly took him past the jewelry store on the way to another destination. Finally when he returned, the credit was intact, and the old man had returned to Europe. He also discovered a pearl engagement ring perfectly and beautifully suited for his intended bride, the one he was confident he could be God's best for.

Chapter 16: The Vintage Friend

But one thing I do:
Forgetting what is behind
and straining toward what is ahead,
I press on toward the goal to win
the prize for which God has called me
heavenward in Christ Jesus.

Philippians 3:13-15

While walking through the creaky screen door or even the heavy wooden one that followed, there would be no mistaking the smell of musty decay fused with a permanent suggestion of stale urine, much like you'd find in a dilapidated nursing home. It was dark and barely lit, and the hardwood floor squeaked in unison with the screen door as it closed behind her. The house itself was a typical 1950s ranch, open from the first step into the living area. The hallway to the left led to three bedrooms and a compact bathroom, while the kitchen with a tiny table for two was directly behind the living room.

On the brown sofa, a pile of arthritic joints linking a bundle of brittle bones wrangled together in the final depiction of a used-up old woman. Somewhere between disgrace and weariness, her head had been triggered to hang low with her chin resting on her chest. Her white hair rebelled against earlier brush strokes as it now dangled in selected places about her face and randomly stood rigidly at attention in others. Holding the pile of bones together, a light blue housedress was draped from her fragile shoulders and buttoned haphazardly without recognition of proper uniformity. About her ankles, heavy white socks covered her swollen feet. Woven together in polite solitude, her fingers formed the clasp of her delicate hands with unpolished nails chipped and carelessly torn. Twisted by age, her hands were covered by the thinness of translucent skin that wrinkled about with brown age spots and blotchy purple stains from bruises forbidden to heal.

Vintage to the core, the unfortunate woman had the distinction of outliving all her contemporaries born in the early 1900s. Surviving at a paltry level, far below poverty, she lived in a home owned by the niece of a best friend, who had been deceased for nearly twenty years. The months, years, and decades had gone by more quickly then she was able to prepare for them. Instead she busied herself, living her life to the fullest until she no longer could.

Now suffering from dementia manifesting itself in terrorizing hallucinations, she was also mostly blind from macular degeneration, able to hear only marginally when the volume was turned up on a twenty-year-old device and limited in mobility from the ravages of arthritis, peripheral edema, and who knew what else. Yet each morning the vintage woman hoisted her sad pile of bones from bed, bathed as properly as she was able, fed unidentifiable food scraps to her peculiar and aloof cat, prepared a cup of instant coffee to compliment a piece of dry toast, and then waited. She waited for anyone to arrive, someone who would interject even a morsel of sanity into the dementia hallucinations.

The door squeaked as she walked in. Unprepared and reluctant to actually involve herself beyond what was called for by good manners, she greeted the vintage woman with an uneasy hello. She wasn't completely sure how her girlfriend, the niece, had charmed her into checking on the elderly woman in between leaving the office and meeting for dinner. Gently coaxed by the assurances it would only take a couple minutes, she was determined for it to be so. Only a few minutes behind this quick stop, the niece and her planned to enjoy a bit of fine dining, a delightful glass of wine, and the expected girlfriend chatter. The smell of the house was hideous, and the darkness was foreboding.

"How are you doing today?" She took her place on the ottoman situated in front of where the vintage woman waited.

Replicating the performance of imaginary strings pulling into place by a puppeteer, the vintage woman uncoiled into an erect, prim, and proper posture afforded upon arrival for the queen of England herself. The elegance was startling.

"Oh my dear, do you have blonde hair? It is beautiful. I can almost see you. And the smell of your perfume, it is delightful." Her words sounded a nearly rehearsed melody.

"Thank you. Yes, I do have blonde hair."

She watched the vintage woman carefully try to follow the sound of her voice, leaning forward with outreached hands, seeking hungrily for something affectionate to grasp. Obliging, she gently stroked the backs of the old woman's hands. It wasn't pity, care, or even a desire to be comforting that moved her to tenderness. Amidst the smell, the darkness, and the crumpled bones, she felt a sweet spirit within the vintage woman sink dreadfully close to her own. For a split second, it was perfect, peaceful, and precious.

"Are you here to stop the water?" the vintage woman asked with a full-blown dose of polite agitation.

"The water?" She was uncertain if she'd heard properly.

"Yes, can't you see it?" she continued with gnawing anxiety. "The house is turning upside down because of the voices coming from the basement. Go over to the register and listen. You can hear them burning the house in small places. Once the ball stopped bouncing around my bed, water came to drench the flames. You must tell them to leave now!" the vintage woman begged fearfully. "Please, please can you make them go away?"

"Oh my. I'm sorry, but I don't know what I can do." She looked toward the ornamental grate covering the hole in the wall where the furnace in the basement would blow air. "Are you sure there is water?"

"Yes! Yes! It will drown me while I'm asleep if the refrigerator doesn't electrocute me first. I unplugged it because the voices told me to leave the door open and let the frost out of the freezer. They want to steal the cold air." The terror in her voice was as frightening as she was fearful.

"It's okay, sweetie. I'll do my best. They must make it awful for you." She stroked her hand. "Let me go check on it for you. Is that okay?"

"Yes, yes. You go check, and I'll stay right here." The old woman nodded her head several times.

She leaned forward, kissed the vintage woman on the forehead, patted her hands, and then stood up from the place on the ottoman before looking in the kitchen. The refrigerator door was open. The electrical cords to the stove, refrigerator, and toaster were all unplugged and hanging across the counter. A can of half-eaten cat food was dumped over on the table, and the water bowl was empty.

After arranging everything back into proper order, she returned to her place on the ottoman. "I took care of it. You are safe now," she told her.

"Oh, you are such a miracle! An angel! I don't know if I would have survived through the night if you hadn't shown up to rescue me. Those voices are mean to me. Aren't you afraid of them?" The vintage woman relaxed into the aftermath of temporary safety.

"Maybe a little. But it's going to be okay now. Don't you worry" She knew the voices would return with the fire, bouncing balls, water, or whatever the vintage woman's dementia would summon.

For this abrupt and brief moment, they shared the quiet of respite back to the perfect, peaceful, and precious. It was the nature of dementia to swing beyond ordinary manners of a new introduction into the details of torment and then back again.

In the movement of the swings lay an invitation to forget the hallucinations and reminisce about the past. The vintage woman described her life when she was young, working at the *Chicago Tribune* as a copywriter during the late 1930s until the end of the 1950s. She took the train rides between Northern and Central Illinois to visit friends and family. She told how Macy's had the best shoe department with a certain handsome salesman taking a shine to her whenever she shopped.

"High heels are the best exercise for your legs, you know! Nothing short of dancing all day will keep them near as lovely. And don't worry about your feet. Soak them at night in Epson salts, and they'll be just fine. By the time they start giving you real fits, you'll be too old for pretty shoes anyway."

They compared notes on dresses and styles of the era, designers with a real appreciation for the feminine silhouette, and how being a woman was a much better deal than being a man, every day all day. In all of it, the vintage woman skirted the part of the story when she was married to a man who beat her and how ugly it was to be divorced during a time in history when women were judged harshly for not having a husband. She also left out the hard places about longing to have a child or how devastated she was when her longtime boyfriend died suddenly in a train accident. The layers of heartbreak each time she buried a friend, were systematically buried along side them. Then ultimately she privately neglected to reveal how it felt to lose herself to the end of life as a stranger wasting into a bag of old bones and terrorized by dementia. As much as anything, the vintage woman missed herself.

Hastily a bond between the two of them matured through the ritual of one evening during the week and Sunday afternoons when she brought special meals created from obscure recipes. She learned aging had not hindered the vintage woman's sense of taste, as it often came with advice or hints for tweaking the flavors. Restless from hallucinations, her lucidity was rare and sporadic, brief, and often times fraught with emotional tangles.

She began to mirror the waiting game. As the vintage woman waited for a guest to arrive, she waited for the vintage woman of old to break through the madness. The stranger who routinely greeted her was not the woman she cared so deeply and yearned to know. Despite the horror of it, the vintage woman was able to delicately touch a vulnerable place within her she hid from the world and dared not acknowledge, even in her own darkness. Leaving was always the cruelest part of their visits.

The days when no respite from the hallucinations materialized, she was haunted by the notion it would come moments after she left. And on the other days, she carried through the creaky door a sorrowful longing for the periods when the vintage woman's charm would last just a bit longer. Either way, the hollowness of leaving seemed selfish.

Out of sync with their usual routine, she nonchalantly stopped by midafternoon on a Wednesday. The living room was empty apart from where the cat lounged on the back of the sofa.

"Hello. It's me," she announced. She heard nothing.

Without a response to ward off the tightening of her stomach, she gingerly walked toward the kitchen, eager to find her safe. She had only seen the vintage woman away from her waiting position during the times she coaxed her to eat lunch at the small table for two. Her absence from the sofa seemed peculiar.

Yet it wasn't. It was in the rhythm of the vintage woman's day. Each afternoon at the same time, she prepared herself another cup of instant coffee. Today was simply the day she would be watched, in quiet, the painstaking efforts it would take. Fumbling about the counter to find the electrical cord for the stove, running her hands along the wall to find the outlet, the vintage woman held the cord in one hand as she moved it toward the other hand, holding the place by the outlet. Cautiously she plugged one into the other. Bending down as she balanced with one hand gripping the bottom cupboard, she brought a small pan out from the drawer, gently banging it on the counter until the noise changed when the sound of tapping on Formica turned to the metal of the sink. Her fumbling continued as she splashed water into the pan, placed it on the burner, and chose a knob to turn onto high.

The vintage woman counted to three as she traced her way across the upper cupboards until she found a handle to the one holding the instant coffee, a single cup, and a teaspoon. Twisting the top from the jar, she measured out two scoops with the spoon, resting it in the cup as she closed the jar of coffee. And she waited.

Today for the first time, she was sadly awestruck by the simple actions the vintage woman wrestled with through demons, hallucinations, terrorizing fear, and how far the journey to make of simple cup of coffee would challenge her beloved friend. It was a stark reality she hadn't considered. While she waited, sometimes endlessly for the craziness to subside enough to enjoy a chat, the vintage woman was battling through the terror to get there.

In stillness as she leaned on the door jamb watching, questions began to seep from the contrast of where they each stood. "*How many times had she herself let difficult challenges convince her it wasn't worth the trouble or found enough faults in something that she gave up? Even harsher, how often had she been overwhelmed to the point of dismissing the merit of something because she didn't feel confident she could pay the price? She had left love on the sidelines because she was far too anxious to move on instead of pausing to explore it.*" This vintage woman who lived side by side with the menacing stranger lurking about had forced her to wait even when it wasn't worth it.

"Hi, it's me. Can I help you finish?" she asked.

"Oh my goodness! You startled me! I am so glad you are here. It's a miracle you know! The voices have been chanting about a zebra coming from the zoo to cause trouble. They will be here any moment. You should hurry, or you will get caught by the electricity," the vintage woman rambled.

She helped her shuffle over to the small table, fluffed the dirty yellow gingham cushion on the seat, and tenderly helped her to sit. While the vintage woman continued rambling, she finished making the proper cup of coffee, and in line with how the vintage woman insisted, she also reluctantly prepared one for herself.

"I have a question for you," she softly tested, not being sure if the vintage woman sitting across the small table had enough clarity to answer. "Every little thing you do is so challenging. Why - or should I say where - do you find the inspiration to face your days?"

"Oh my sweetie, I hardly face them. The days come, and then they go," the vintage woman said, acquiescing to what seemed to be the richness of futility.

Still not sure if the vintage woman were coherent or not, she pressed, "But I was watching you try to make a cup of coffee. Everything you needed to do was so difficult. Was it worth the trouble?"

"No, not really. This is crummy coffee. It doesn't matter how well you or even I prepare it. It will always still be a crummy cup of coffee. You see, when it is all measured, this life is not worth it. I wish I could tell you all the joys outweighed all the heartache. But that wouldn't be the truth. Not today anyway."

"So why do you try so hard then?"

"Because only by the mighty, powerful, and unfathomable hand of God ..." she trailed off for a few seconds, stirred her coffee, and waited for time to catch up. "I still can."

Chapter 17: The Auditor

Every good and perfect gift is from above,
coming down from the Father
of the heavenly lights,
who does not change
like shifting shadows.

James 1:17

The oblong black serving tray contained the only boundaries among the piles of papers scattered about the long, mahogany conference room table. On the tray, four glass tumblers and several bottles of water in varying degrees of fullness surrounded a matching half-empty ice bucket, all taken for granted. None of it was offered with hospitality, but rather with the half heartedness of good manners and obligation. Remarkably the stacks of paper formed a scene emulating the view seen through the floor-to-ceiling windows of the twenty-first story and out onto the rooftops of dirty building also built in piles. Apart from the controlled chaos on the mahogany table, the room was spotlessly cleaned, neat and otherwise comfortable in an elegantly simple style without the adornments of wealth or prosperity. It was tasteful. Various colored Post-it notes marked the identity on many of the piles with scratchy handwritten codes only decipherable by the author of each.

It had been a two-year investigation. Today would be his last meeting. As an auditor for the Securities and Exchange Commission (SEC), he would leave every piece of paper behind for someone else to tend to. It was his role to find corruption or, in its absence, create some from the slightest hint of a misstep. Specializing in nonprofit organizations with support from outside investors, this would be the first time he reluctantly left empty-handed. Cleaning up the aftermath it created was not for his consideration. He simply wanted to leave it behind and forget his failure.

With the mastery of a well-respected leader in his profession, scouring through the details from years of business transactions, emails, documentation, and contracts should have provided the inevitable discrepancy eventually found by his team. Something - anything - he could use to prove an infraction had occurred. Whether intentional or not, the result would be the same.

Nonetheless this case bothered him. Initially he was convinced a deep inquiry into the business practices would be another easy win for the department. The organization being examined was relatively small and run by a team of businesspeople who had ventured beyond their professions into nonprofit work for underserved countries. They were led by the vision of a woman who believed they could help change the course of the future by teaching others how to provide for themselves. He was certain the success of their efforts must be flawed.

As the details began to unfold, finding any error became increasingly challenging until his motivation was driven by fierceness rather than commitment to find the truth. There was simply no worldly explanation how this organization could stand up to the scrutiny his department held and effortlessly wielded.

Two years of his life had been for naught. As he considered all the time committed by him and his team, the endless hours and resources dedicated to finding what should have been a simple needle in the haystack, he dropped his head in weariness, shaking it from side to side. He was not ready to give up. Strolling around the mahogany table, he randomly flipped through papers trying to find one last hint. It wasn't there.

Pulling a cellphone from the breast pocket of his gray pinstripe suit, he called the office of another team leader for the department. While the phone on the other end rang, he gazed down at the polish on his wingtip shoes, put his right hand in the pocket of his trousers, and walked over to the window where his back would be facing toward the closed door. It was the only privacy he would be afforded. Looking beyond the other buildings, he gazed at the blue sky and saw nothing.

"Are you sure we are done here?" he asked. "Can you think of anything else?" After listening to the answer, he replied, "Okay, I guess I'll let them know we are closing the file and ending the inquiry. Am I still within the regs to tell them it is provisional with a ninety-day waiting period? You're right. What's the point? Go ahead and get the closing letter prepared. I'll give you a call when I get to the airport. Thanks, pal!"

The blue of the sky began to come into focus as he noted only one small cloud in the distance inhibited its otherwise flawlessness. Returning the phone to his pocket, he paused, trying to frame the words he would say before he left. "*Should he apologize or defend the efforts of the SEC? Or should he offer a flimsy rationalization why the past two years had been valuable to either side?*" On a real level, he naïvely wanted to simply excuse himself to the men's room and not return or say anything. As much as he knew the impact it had on his team, he couldn't fathom how it must have affected the organization or people who had been treated with callousness.

"Innocent until proven guilty," he had heard the haunting words from his grade school teacher as she taught the intricacies of the fourteenth amendment to the Constitution. It had

been far too long since he considered anyone's innocence. Right or wrong, it was his job to orchestrate the instrument of guilt.

The reeling of his thoughts was interrupted as he heard the door to the conference room open. Turning from the window, he saw the woman who first forecast the vision for the organization entering the room. She was distinguished-looking, perhaps in her mid-fifties and close to five-foot four. With fashionably styled gray hair cut short, it rested tucked behind each ear, and a wisp of bangs nearly touched her eyelashes. Her eyes were remarkably bluer than he remembered. He noticed she was dressed simply in a gray, long-sleeved tunic with matching slacks, her only adornment was a simple gold necklace with a charm in the shape of a cross resting just below the third button. Her face and eyes were uncommonly peaceful. There was a casual sophistication about her movements, gentle yet steadfast. She extended her hand for a customary greeting, and he noticed a thin gold watch about her wrist.

"Good afternoon, I understand you are coming close to wrapping things up for the day?" she asked as they shook hands.

He recognized her from their brief meeting at the beginning of the investigation. All communications since that time had been through attorneys, well-rehearsed staff, or emails. Encountering her today wasn't what he expected.

"Yes, I think we have everything we need." He stopped short of telling her they were at a conclusion for the investigation.

"I'm pleased to hear that. I trust you have had your questions answered properly with full cooperation from my staff?" she prompted for more finality.

"Yes, they have been very helpful. Thank you."

"My assistant informed me she scheduled a taxi to the airport for you. Will you be leaving this afternoon?"

"Yes, my flight takes off in about two hours."

"Then would you mind spending a few minutes chatting with me?" She gestured to the two chairs positioned on either side of the corner at the end of the mahogany conference table.

"No, not at all. I have a few minutes." He felt anxious about such a casual request in light of the contentiousness he sensed they shared.

Moving from his stance by the window, he cautiously took the seat facing the door. In response, she took the one with her back to it.

Casually folding her hands to rest on the table in front of her, she leaned forward very slowly. "Tell me. Where do we go from here?"

With the full weight of disappointment lurking in the staunchness of his tone, he said, "I believe the investigation has come to a conclusion. A letter will be prepared and sent to your attorney within a few days."

It was over.

"Aaah, then I have indeed been informed correctly. Thank you for your directness. It is kind of you to let me know." Her cadence continued with the same poise as her appearance.

He began to appreciate the etiquette entwined within her genuineness and the formality of her gentleness.

"It pleases me we have been able to put the SEC's concerns to rest."

"It's been a long haul for all of us," he gingerly replied.

"I appreciate all the work you and your associates have devoted toward clearing our reputation of any allegations."

"Had she completely missed the point?" he thought. They were dedicated to proving quite the opposite. It was disturbing to hear her now thank him for the very investigating they dedicated to finding the organization had criminal intentions. Finding anything out of the ordinary, anything would have certainly meant proceeding toward prosecution, stopping the charity work, and permanently closing the doors. It

wasn't his intention to clear her but indict her. And certainly, in his mind, didn't make sense she would thank him.

"We just want to find the truth, ma'am." He fumbled with his discomfort.

"Truth?" she asked quietly.

"Yes, we want to find the truth," he repeated.

"Then do you mind if I explain a part of the truth that hasn't been requested during the investigation?" she sympathetically probed.

"I'm not sure it is in your best interest or if it will make any difference," he cautioned.

"Perhaps not, but I'd like to try if you don't mind," she pressed just a little deeper.

"All right, if you insist." He looked toward the window, wanting to leave.

Beyond his departure, he didn't want to know the truth about the actions of the last two years. Convinced she would try to assign guilt for doing his job, he blocked any openness he might have felt for knowing the rest. He had done a good job, even if the result weren't what was intended. He would give her only a couple of dismissive minutes to explain, excuse himself, and then leave. After all he had a plane to catch.

"How long have you been working for the SEC?" she asked.

"Twelve years," he sounded uncharacteristically defensive when he spoke.

"Hmmm, indeed. That is just a bit longer than when I founded this organization. It sounds like we were both on the same path to get here, one way or another." She paused for a few seconds. "I was a corporate attorney for a long time, specializing in performing audits and representing my clients in anticipation or defense of any investigations they may have. When God called me to leave private practice and start this nonprofit organization, I knew what the rules were. Do you understand? I was equipped and prepared to do everything in accordance not simply with the law but in conjunction with God's plan. To protect it from harm."

He nodded his head.

"You see, if I did not honor the blessings God provided to do His work, in my mind, it would have been the same as me disgracing Him. In doing so, it would not simply be myself I affected or harmed, but all those who depend on God for the provision supplied through this work. All the families in the isolated countries who can now earn a living to support themselves would have been betrayed. This is a generational work. The parents pass down to their children not only a skill but hope for a future. Which quite frankly, we wouldn't be able to offer apart from the mighty, powerful, and unfathomable hand of God. Nothing I would ever know or want for myself could ever be as important. I wouldn't willingly jeopardize it," she explained.

Trying to justify his position, he responded, "You have to know, in my line of work, what you describe is not just the exception to the rule. It is completely contradictory to anything I've experienced." Then he felt it. The tugging at his heart pulled him from the staunch defensive posture of an investigator to the full-blown human side of empathizing. "I'm sorry if it has been difficult for you and your staff."

"Thank you." She paused. "It has been a time where everyone has learned something remarkable about how he or she fits into this work. I'm not going to kid you. It has been a grueling test for each of us in our own unique way. Yet in all of it, God has gracefully guided us. And we've come out of it in a stronger place. Let me explain something. To defend ourselves during the investigation, resources of time, attention, heartache, and a great deal of money have all flown through this office like the wind. Amazing amounts. God provided those too. All of it comes from Him. Every good and perfect gift."

"Are you telling me you believe the investigation was a gift?" he asked.

"Indeed! Think about it. The SEC has proven to anyone who cares to ask that our business practices are irreproachable, quite an accomplishment in the world of nonprofit organizations these days. And over the last two years, we continued to thrive under the scrutiny. We learned what we were made of and how to depend on God in new ways. For that, I will happily thank you and your team. You did a good job."

"In light of everything I don't really think saying 'you're welcome' sounds quite right."

She laughed. "Perhaps not. But all the same, I have prayed you would leave our offices knowing us, as well as our work, just a bit more clearly, being confident you did the best job with no second thoughts, and having a sense of accomplishment for God's kingdom too."

"I'm going to have to mull that one over. But thank you."

"Please do. I believe you will find doing your job well means also finding some of the good guys too." She stood and extended her hand for a farewell. "Be well and safe travels."

He shook her hand and followed her to the reception area of the office. Her assistant cheerfully informed him that his taxi was waiting in the circle drive. Once he left, it would be the assistant's responsibility to begin clearing the clutter from the mahogany conference room table. She would be finished even before his plane landed safely.

Chapter 18: The Violinist

David and all the Israelites were celebrating
with all their might before God,
with songs and with harps, lyres,
timbrels, cymbals and trumpets.

1 Chronicles 13:8

Five semicircles of black chairs bordered the wooden platform where the conductor would orchestrate his, or perhaps her, interpretation of how the many instruments, artists, and tiers of energy would mysteriously unite into the legacy of Tchaikovsky's heart. In the second row, third chair from the stage's edge, a tall, handsome violinist suited in tuxedo and tails with a white bowtie fidgeted as he ever so skillfully tuned the turning pegs of his beloved friend, fashioned from the finest wood and four open strings. Cloaked in the intensity streaming from his blue eyes, concentration wrinkled his brow with deliberate preparation for what was to come. He knew the possibilities.

It was spring. The air outside was light with a fragrant mist tempting one to hesitate before leaving the budding of nightfall being born from a hectic day. Yet through the massive doors laden with intricately woven grandeur, the anticipation lay hopeful for an even nobler image of God's splendor. Night could be reserved for after. The audience began to fill the symphony hall, shuffling to find a prearranged respite identified by the ticket in hand, marked with a row and seat. For her, it was DD9. Through the door on the south side, into an aisle leading to the familiar course where she would turn left toward the front, the third seat of the fourth row waited open for her arrival.

Politely she made a brief introduction with the couple now seated to her left in DD7 and DD8. The woman, plainly unadorned, was eager to announce herself as a structural engineer, and she supposed the man accompanying her was in the music industry. With vibrant turquoise-rimmed glasses, a camel-colored sports jacket, jeans, and cowboy boots, while outwardly unexpected, he nevertheless wore the industry uniform. To her right, an elderly couple crumpled into aging seemed fearful of disruption. Their journey to DD10 and DD11 may have been one of resilience. She honored their privacy.

Opening the program brochure, she coveted the next few minutes to learn what she could during the brief pause before the concert began. The activity surrounding her, intensified by the chatter of fellow patrons, was a well-fought distraction. She had not come to belong in the audience, but to discover the music. Committing to the season of classical symphonies had been an impulsive decision grown from a yearning to step beyond the box where her solace had betrayed her.

Despite quietly smiling each time she saw her calendar denoted the commitment, with dreadful consistency the hours leading up to her arrival were fraught with interruption. Today had been no less a challenge, leaving her to make a series of excuses to the girlfriend she urged to substitute in her DD9 place. In saying it was for the very reasons she used as justifications to avoid attending, her girlfriend declined the invitation and encouraged her to be steadfast in her commitment to go. Indeed each of the interruptions, excuses, and even the spring night would be asked to wait. Flipping to the page of the program where her introduction to Tchaikovsky would be unlocked, she sighed into the printed words.

Feeling the heaviness of someone else's gaze, she looked up, ever so fleetingly exchanging a glance with the violinist. The distance between them made it awkward to discern if it were she he saw or the myriad of nameless faces marrying into one congregation. He looked away into the distance and then back to his beloved friend tenderly held with the lower end leaning on his thigh and the neck tilting close to his left shoulder.

Three precisely refined, crystal clear chimes breached the clamor from the audience, lights dimmed, and silence fell. Only a few brief moments of silence broke the commotion of many. It was startling how the bustling of the audience was instantly paralyzed in hypnosis. Breaths were held, eyes riveted, and all senses beyond that of listening ceased or, at the very least, for now were abandoned. The hurried footsteps of the conductor darting toward the platform signaled the time had come.

Facing the orchestra, taking a deep breath, and storing the air in his lungs for an endless second, he raised his arms, holding a baton in his right hand. He lingered and then stampeded into Tchaikovsky.

Suddenly the thrill of the symphony erupted. The black chairs were saturated with vigorous testimony to the hours turned into a lifetime of practiced affection for one thing, an intercourse dedicated to revealing the mystery of how God transformed passion into sound.

Each of the performers knew, intimately and without recognition by the audience, precisely the journey taken to this one fleeting point in time. She wondered if they also knew for an instant how the mighty, powerful, and unfathomable hand of God committed their efforts to those witnessing it, the very ones who indeed journeyed to the same place in time without recognition by the performers. It seemed mightier than the combination of the symphony hall, the artists, the audience, and even this particular spring evening. Still between the orchestra and the listeners, an obstacle of distance at the edge of the stage marked who would give to the sound and who would take from it, so much like the Father and His beloved creation, an eternity of giving and receiving to each other across sacred divides.

The violinist was gracious in his contribution. At ease in his posture, the pensiveness of his brow now absorbed the instructions of the sheet music with steady, even strokes drawing his bow across, pointing in flawless synchronicity with the others to the air above their heads and back again. His hands were gentle, strong, and warm as the ligaments flexed from decades of holding the bow as it danced solo with his beloved wooden friend. With his left hand moving across the fingerboard of the violin, his right alternated between gliding the bow and fervent plucking of the strings. Bobbing his head in unison to the movement of the sound, from time to time he slightly rounded his back forward before sitting up straighter, straining to the edge of the black chair until the intensity of the music allowed him to relax again. The seriousness of his expression was occasionally disrupted as a smile of accomplishment slipped out upon the finish of a crescendo. And once his segment of the sound calmed, the chin rest served as remnants to a boyhood resting place for his head on a pillow. Steadily watching the conductor, the sheet music, and those around him, the violinist entrusted the sound to the audience and to her.

Across a couple hundred years from Tchaikovsky's heart, through the interwoven lives of the artists, the audience, and her improbable presence was the passion transforming into sound. For her, it seemed if there were a point where the completeness of it originated, God's gift must have come through the violinist and his finest wooden friend.

Lingering closely from DD9, she reminded herself to breathe. And for those intimate moments, she closed her eyes to feel the weight of it surrounding her. Seeping out from around it, the other instruments stood back while the violinist played to center stage, nowhere to go beyond more. In the darkness behind her closed eyes, the decorations in her imagination reeled with greatness, and the silence of immense sound peacefully erased the specifics of everything else within her world.

She followed the music amidst an illusion of Tchaikovsky's heart and into his desires -across the landscape of his voyage, up the encounters of hills, and swaying back to the dance only he heard for the first time. There was no distinguishable delineation between where she stopped and the music began, for in the very briefness of it, she became the sound, and the sound became her. Her story unfolded among his, both Tchaikovsky's and the violinist as one, who in return granted her an alternative translation of her own. The bridge between reality and splendor vanished into the music.

Far too soon it became more then she could hold. Upon opening her eyes, the world was still close. The kindness of his hands was the only clarity within her line of sight, yet the audience, the conductor, the orchestra, and the other violinists sitting around him were all still vividly near, beautiful and extraordinary, until, as the sound concluded and silence again fell for an instant, a deep, heavy unmistakable sigh of relief signaled the violinist recognized he had done well.

First unconsciously tickling the side of his forehead with the bow and then flicking the strain from his wrist, he waited for the conductor to gesture toward his section of the orchestra to stand and receive the explosion of the audience applause. She stood with the others, smiling and nodding her head with the program neatly tucked under her arm. The sound was now hers to give back. The violinist appeared weary, or perhaps it was a sense of relief, well-being, and accomplishment.

Somewhere between the world and eternity lies a bridge, fleeting, mysterious, and sacred nearly to the point of being incomprehensible until one capriciously stumbles across.

For in this moment, she had encountered a foretaste of it. Captured within the magnitude of time, lives, experiences, and this very performance was God introducing the artists to the audience, the audience to the artists, and both to what could come.

The violinist looked toward DD9. They caught each other's gaze. She nodded. He smiled. They each turned in opposite directions, following the purposes of their own path to greet the fragrance of another spring night.

Chapter 19: The Nurse

Surely your goodness
and love will follow me
all the days of my life,
and I will dwell in the
house of the Lord forever.

Psalm 23:6

She thought he looked adorable, popping his attention back and forth between driving and petting Rowdy, their black lab riding half in the backseat with his front quarters and paws languishing over the armrest between the two of them. The years had been kind to her husband. His eyes were a bit turned down on the edges with a few wrinkles accentuating how his skin wasn't as taut as it had once been. The coloring of his cheeks had somewhat faded into an ashen hue on the places of his face framed by the two-day stubble of growth from a beard, gray as his hair. The broad shoulders she first laid her head on now slumped from decades of wearing the weight of their world. Many years she believed the sparkle in his eyes would never return. But there it was, reminding her, from behind the blue, his spirit was still as young as it had been forty years earlier on this very day.

She remembered it clearly, as if a gift to be periodically unwrapped anytime memories were needed to fill in gaps when intimacy seemed distant. On their wedding night, they lay peacefully in the dark, waiting for the next sunrise to pronounce to the world. Indeed it was true. They were now husband and wife. While she sheepishly hid beneath the covers cuddled close under his arm, he fondly kissed her forehead. He chattered on, describing the plans he had for the life they would share, uncharacteristic for the quiet fellow she believed him to be. In those first moments, he promised her someday down the road they would take a trip across the United States, exploring all the wonderful places they could only dream about on their first night together.

"Someday down the road" converted their dream into an anthem they recited hundreds, if not thousands, of times. The youthful spirit they saved could not stay the years from relentlessly speeding past. Today she nodded her head in appreciation for the irony in "down the road" had not escaped her.

Just as he planned, they enjoyed a good life. It had not been trouble-free. Certainly in forty years they had come face-to-face with many curveballs, disasters, and setbacks. Yet he hung in there with her just as she did with him. Two grown children, three grandbabies, a paid mortgage, and a retirement promising a life of leisure was now theirs to cash in on. To celebrate, they took the early dreams and ventured from their hometown in Vermont to see as much of America as they could possibly stand and more.

New York City delivered a dreadful play on off-off-off Broadway. Laughing about their good taste in theatre, they headed toward the Liberty Bell in Philadelphia. Shopping on Michigan Avenue in Chicago proved a delightful exercise in spending nearly a hundred dollars on what others may consider next to nothing, but they cherished as treasures. After Mount Rushmore in South Dakota and Yellowstone in Montana, they found themselves drinking wine until they were downright silly in Napa Valley, California. After meeting a couple friendly men in northern Texas, they traveled across the red clay in Oklahoma toward Tennessee to compare cowboys to country boys. With a smirk from under the wide rim of a black signature cowboy hat, they were told there was a difference, even if the hats looked the same. Honky-tonking down Broadway, Second Avenue, and River Front Park in Nashville proved the Texans were right. Music City was indeed wonderfully different.

As the sun was beginning to set on the summer evening, they decided to put in a few hours on the last leg of their trip toward home, north on highway 65. Her husband was still laughing about the Elvis impersonator introducing them to Forrest Gump on the sidewalk in front of Tootsies. It struck her how long it had been since she saw him relaxed, laughing, and flat-out enjoying life. Yes, retirement was good for him. With one hand resting casually on Rowdy's head, petting behind his right ear, and the other on the steering wheel, her husband turned, winked at her, smiled, and then looked back toward the road in front of them.

Terror sharply slapped across his face as his eyes instantly widened beyond anything recognizable. Before she was able to record what she was witnessing, everything went black.

Fifteen steps outside the hospital room, a nurse with long auburn hair loosely tied up in a knot, leaving random pieces to punctuate the urgency of her posture, held a phone to her ear as she paced in front of the nurse's station. Her blue scrubs fit loosely over a flowered tank top with her running shoes matching the purple that peeked out from the V neckline. She unconsciously tapped her forehead just above the square, wire-framed glasses shielding her blue eyes and contrasting against her pale ivory skin, marked only by a hint of cosmetics.

"Yes, I know it is late." She paused. "22:14 to be exact. I don't care what time it is. I'm telling you there is a dog out there running scared. I believe it is a black lab that will answer to Rowdy. You have to find it and get it here to me as soon as possible." Pausing again, she listened. "Of course it is important. I can assure you it is the most important thing you are going to do all week!" There was another pause. "I'm not going to listen to any excuses. If you don't get that dog and get it here now, you will find out exactly how angry I can get." There was yet another pause. "Thank you. That's all I wanted to hear. I'm in ICU. I'll call down to security in the ER and tell them you will be coming. Thank you. This really means a lot."

In room 312, she tried to open her eyes. The pressure in her chest felt like a seven-story building collapsing on top of her. She could faintly hear the beeping of a monitor as it recorded her heart beating and the pressure of her blood. Compressions from a ventilator hissed rhythmically in unison with the beeping. A sharp pain reverberated throughout her right side as she twisted to lift her shoulder. She wasn't able to move. The tube inserted down her throat to open her airways made it painfully impossible to groan. Consumed by the numbness, she surrendered, slipping back into unconsciousness.

An hour and fifteen minutes later, the nurse took a call from security, notifying her a police officer was on his way up with the dog. Stepping from the elevator, Rowdy fearfully hesitated to follow the lead of the leash held by the officer. With his tail behind his legs, ears tucked close and down, and an arch in his back, the dogs eyes were somber.

Walking toward them, the nurse knelt to pet him, kissing his head and gently caressing his shoulders. "It's gonna be okay, fella. I promise." She signed the documents to release the animal into her care and then turned to walk toward room 312.

"A dog! We can't have a dog in ICU!" she heard over her shoulder from the familiar voice of *that* nurse.

"Why not?" she asked.

"Because! You don't know what it will do."

"Like what?"

"Well, like it could do its business in the middle of the room or something."

"You're kidding me, right? I've helped clean up brain matter from floors, blood, guts, severed body parts, and all variations of trauma, and you think a little dog poop is going to make a big difference?" She was beginning to feel the anger seeping in again.

"Well, if you don't take that dog outside, I'm going to write you up."

"Knock yourself out! I'll be happy to explain my actions to the review board. But it won't be happening tonight, so just stay out of our way."

Her focus was now on room 312. With Rowdy resting by her side, she slumped down into the chair reserved for family members or visitors. It had been a long day. Playing out in her head the responses she would give the review board, she also remembered a cutting remark she heard from her stepmother at lunch the day before. As a nurse for a dermatologist, she held little respect or understanding of the ICU.

"All you do is hook bodies up to machines. You should try a homeopathic method of healing instead."

Tonight as she sat waiting with Rowdy by her side, she was grateful for not having dignified the statement with a response. "*There simply is too much ignorance in the world*," she thought.

She also knew it was best for everyone if she shook it off. Worrying about "what if" would not change the "what is."

Her attention diverted to the woman trying to open her eyes again. First she began blinking very groggily and then with increased intention. Rowdy vaulted from the floor onto the bed, licking her face around the tube. There was no mistaking the woman was now fully conscious. She could identify the nurse standing by her side and again hear the machines working. The room was painted bright white, and the lights were dimmed. Nudging Rowdy, the nurse moved him over to rest by her side.

Leaning closer, intently looking in each other's eyes, the nurse spoke gently, "You're okay. There was an accident, and you're in the hospital. We're taking good care of you. We had to put an intubation tube in your throat to help you breathe so you won't be able talk right now. I'm guessing this is your dog, Rowdy. Can you nod your head for me?"

She felt the nurse stroking her arm.

"Good sign," the nurse thought.

Nodding was easier than she imagined it would be. Looking around the room, she searched to find where her husband was waiting. Exploring back and forth, she was able to effortlessly move her head. She couldn't see him. Trying to talk, she heard a vague grunt come from her tube.

"No, no. Don't try to talk. Are you looking for your husband?" Understanding her patient when he and she couldn't speak had grown to be an instinctual gift God provided both. Nodding she was grateful, the nurse understood.

Sitting on the opposite side of the bed, the nurse gently held her hand. "Sweetie, I'm so sorry, but he didn't make it. We did everything we could, but his injuries were very severe, and he died shortly after arriving here. I was with him in the end, and he wasn't in any pain. He asked me to find Rowdy for you. And the last thing he said was to let you know he loved you bigger than the whole country. You are a wonderful mother, and he wanted you to live."

At that moment, the tube down her throat prevented the scream she did not need to hear coming from the deepest places of her soul. The weight on her chest was hardly significant compared to the immensity of the blow now ravaging her otherwise numb body. She began to shiver. Tears were streaming down the side of her temple. Rowdy lay quietly beside her.

The nurse placed another blanket over her and her beloved pet, wiping away the wetness from her tears. "I've spoken with your son. He and your daughter are on their way here. They will be arriving early in the morning. We're going to get you through this. I promise you, by the mighty, powerful, and unfathomable hand of God, we will get you through this. For now, I'm going to put some medication in your IV to help you rest. Rowdy and I are going to stay right here with you until you wake up."

Morning came hours before she awoke. The nurse and Rowdy stood guard over her sorrow. Opening her eyes, she saw her family mingling about her room: both of her children with their spouses, her younger brother, his wife, and her sister, the best friend she had loved and followed from birth. Each had been weeping and praying for her.

Chapter 20: The Woman on the Beach

And I pray that you,
being rooted and established in love,
may have power,
together with all the Lord's holy people,
to grasp how wide and long and high
and deep is the love of Christ,
and to know this love that surpasses knowledge
that you may be filled to the measure of
all the fullness of God.

Ephesians 3:17-19

She came to the beach for one reason and one reason only, to erase her life by walking into the waves and not coming out. Every detail had been meticulously planned. The messy places of this and that in her house had finally been organized with the laundry actually hanging where it belonged in the closet. Her last will and testament was painstakingly updated. Bills were paid. Anyone she wanted to say good-bye to had unknowingly wished her well before she left for the seven-hour drive toward the ocean. It looked as if she'd prepared her life for a holiday party, polished and pristine. The idea of someone who thought they knew her, seeing anything out of order, would have also witnessed a story she was not willing to leave behind. So she tidied as much of her life as she could, imagining the assumptions. There was even a phase when the speculation of others averted the seriousness of her decision. Nevertheless with time, as all the other distractions she latched onto for significance had done, it slowly wore off too.

Her life had been a long series of misfortune and tragedies. If the timeline were laid out objectively, one would scratch his or her head in wonderment as to how so much could have befallen any one person. Much of it had innocently happened to her with only small portions being self-imposed.

"You should read the book of Job!" those who heard but a glimpse would tell her.

She had. And it made her reconsider trusting the one true God, if He indeed handed Job over to Satan as a play toy. Then in response to Job's cry to the Lord, it was revealed Job didn't understand the majesty of God. "*Of course not,*" she thought. "*He was created simply to long for the knowing.*"

Job's life alone had been spared, meager at best. After being restored, she wondered if he missed the innocence of believing in God's protection before it was seemingly withdrawn or how it would thereafter taint his joy. In her mind, there was no happy ending.

The journey had helped her find a place of consolation and acceptance within her questions. Knowing the answers would not come this side of eternity, had released her curiosity from the toiling aggravation of incessantly seeking. For this she was grateful.

For certain, she held much in gratitude, and she weighed every thread of it carefully. Someone else would always be blessed more than she was and equally as many who were blessed less. It was the natural order of the world she accepted without envy or pride. Hardship would come, crosses would be carried, and suffering was the part of consciousness used to corroborate how well one understood the fallen world. For it was plainly seeing all the cruelty, in more shapes and sizes than even those who suffered, where she could not ignore the truth. Life was a battle. It did not make her despise life, for it reminded her far too much of herself. In all of it, honest, pure goodness fought to survive the onslaught of ugliness with each new day.

Instead it made her yearn for her Yahweh. In the deeply intimate places only God knew best, she longed to be with Him, where she could touch the hem of Christ's garment, feel the grace of forgiveness without fear of another sin, humbly wash His feet clean of the earth, and walk purely and innocently in the Spirit. She craved His mighty, powerful, and unfathomable hand to hold hers without the distance of desire, for the battle to end, and peace to become lasting rather than simply a fleeting glimpse of what was promised. There was nothing the world had left to offer her - not love, not purpose, and not even a quiet place to wait. None of it held enough meaning to dissuade her.

The decision was not made impulsively. She considered as much of it as could be fathomed: the loss, the grief, the judgment, and even the slander. Sadly, alive or not, she faced the very same considerations for herself despite her fate. To ease the aftermath for those who would not understand, were intangible details kneaded sympathetically into how she tidied up her life. In the miracle of praying for them was where she reconciled her choice. She didn't see it as a selfish act. For she had already given all of herself to a life that was now wrung dry and where bitterness inevitably would begin to grow like mold on a discarded rag.

There was nothing left to be selfish about. The stranger she met in mirrors looked outwardly familiar to pictures of the past, dressed in a foreign disguise while it embezzled the intimacy of who she was. The surviving ashes would only oblige a regrettable legacy, breaking her heart and all those who would watch. No explanation she could give would ever erase the misconceptions. So she would leave the questions without a response, spoken, written, or shared in the same place hers would be found, on the other side of eternity.

At midnight in the darkest part of the day, covered in the quietness of slumber, she planned the walk without a witness or interference. The final step of her preparation came a half day before. Noontide was when she introduced herself to the ocean of her destiny as she quietly placed her folding chair in the sand. The irony of it being the Friday after Thanksgiving had not been intentional on her part, nor was it unappreciated. Preparations had simply drawn to a close as the rest of the world swirled in the activity of the holiday. This would be her time spent without the labor of conflicting thoughts, the interruption of life, and the interweaving of relationships.

To be still and know He was God.

Every cliché about the ocean had gone before her, all true. Sitting on the beach, quiet and apart from the bellowing tenor of the waves, she pondered what one last nugget she could learn from it. There was nothing new or out of the ordinary apart from the truly awe-inspiring nature of the waves so far out of her control, the grains of sand far too vast to count, and the warmth of the sun so mysteriously breaking through the coolness of the breeze. The mark where the sand ended and the water began changed every few seconds as the waves continued its ongoing melody with no beginning or end.

Out on the horizon past the waves and miles beyond where she would survive when she ventured out, a straight line unbroken by a single obstruction, precise as the finest point, drew from one side of her place in the sand to the absolute opposite. Above the impenetrably straight line, the sky reached down to meet the glistening water. Somehow the combination of both created a glossy sheen across a patch on the top layers of the water dancing directly in front of her. She supposed sparkling, as a touch of glitter being tossed haphazardly, proved what lie beneath was indeed intended to be special. Without it, one would not know where the earth ended and the sky began, for the blue of both oddly fused simultaneously into a deceitful mirage of one.

The sky was so blue - oh so blue - unmatched and flawless. With the sun positioned in the very center, too bright to look directly toward yet circled by a halo. She could feel it tenderly touch her face with reassurance from further away then even the line of the horizon. The streaming silhouette forming bursts around it reminded her each time she looked that she must look away. Her eyes squinted with strain as she tried again. Yet the sun wouldn't let her see itself.

The briskness of the air caused her to shiver and then roll the cuffs of her trousers back down around her ankles. Her cold, bare feet were burrowed deep until her ankles were covered either with sand or the bottom of her pant legs. She wished she had tossed a scarf into her bag, like the others had done. Instead she pulled the collar of her jacket up close around her neck. The frigidity of the wet air penetrated to the bone even as the sunlight tried to balance it with warmness.

A few yards to her right, a sand castle stood as evidence others had come before her. It was intricately molded, about fifteen feet in diameter, with an imaginative range of levels, layers, and shapes pointing to the efforts of many. It could not have been created in a single day, and she guessed it was an ongoing monument for castle makers and dreamers alike to leave their mark on an otherwise typical beach. She wished them well.

She lingered and contemplated every ounce of it until the cool air could not be held apart from her concentration. Hours had passed. Getting up to leave, she turned and walked to the edge of the water, wondering if it were as cold as the air or if any of the summer warmth remained. On the very tips of her toes, the water was ever as frigid as she supposed until a wave came unexpectedly crashing in. While she looked down at her feet, it bounced beyond her. With it she perceived a slight rise in the temperature. The water was not warm nor was it frigid. "*Yes!*" she thought. She loved the ocean.

In returning to her room, she began tidying up the last details. She wanted the cottage apartment to appear as if it had not been used. It was cozy and delightfully decorated, a place she would visit again if it weren't her last night. Whoever would come into it next would be a stranger, no doubt looking for any hint assuring her safety. Pouring herself a glass of wine, she could not shake the chill she'd gotten at the beach. Wearing an extra pair of fluffy socks, an oversized sweatshirt and raising the thermostat did not provide relief.

The chill had caused her temperature to rise and her body to respond with shivers she could not control. Even though it was only late afternoon, she slipped under the covers of the bed, trying not to muss any corners she'd neatly tucked tight with a signature obsession. The pillows were warm, and she peacefully let her eyes close, believing she would certainly awake before it would be time.

She was wrong. It was morning when the sun woke her with streaming light peeking through the cracks in the window shades. "*Another day*," she thought. She would spend it well. Preparing some breakfast of eggs and toast, she felt good, strong, and determined. There was no hint of disappointment she'd slept through the night. Nor any sense of irony registered with her about how the ocean that God created had interrupted her scheme. She simply plodded on into the day as if it were every bit as intentional as the one before. The only place for her to go was out the cottage door, down the sandy path dotted with flowering shrubs, over the walkway, and back down to the beach. This time she went with a scarf, two shirts under her jacket, canvas shoes filled with thick socks for her feet, and heavier jeans.

As she topped the walkway, looking down toward the water, no one, not a single soul, was on the same beach at the same time on the same day. She was alone, and it made her feel giddy. This was her beach, her day, and her ocean. Almost skipping, she danced toward it and placed her chair in the sand near the edge where the water left a demarcation. It was closer than where she sat the day before. The sand castle had been virtually washed away. "*Someone would build one anew*, she thought. *It would be beautiful again.*"

The air was unquestionably much warmer. Feeling foolish, she began to unravel the scarf wrapped about her neck. Not being enough, she removed her jacket and one of her shirts, rolled up her pant legs to her knee, and then removed her socks and shoes. Today her feet were cooled by the sand instead of covered for warmth. She could feel the heat on her face and discarded any thought of returning for sunscreen. All of it had waited for her return: the same sandy beach, the same glistening horizon, the same tenor of the waves, and the same streaking halo about the sun.

God was the same yesterday, today, and forever.

Settling in, she took a deep breath, exhaling the old air in her lungs and taking in the new. It was when she relaxed that it hit her hard. God was the only one there with her. The whole beach, ocean, sky, sun, the waves, and thunder of the water, ALL of it was for her. Her whole life, with each step taken to get to such a time as this, the miracles of movement fueling her journey, the pain, the joy, the changes, and all the things that stayed the same. Her losses and victories, tragedies and miracles, with every breath brought her to this beach, this day, and this moment, to share alone with God.

She began to weep.

It was too much to comprehend. None of it - every drop of water, every particle of sand, every inch of the blue sky, and the brilliant sun - had any purpose in this place or time apart from her and God. There was not a single living soul other than her. And still she could see and feel it all. As the waves continued to crash in about her, she tried in her humble Job self to grasp how wide and long and high and deep was God's love. She couldn't. Like Job, she was not created to know. She was created to long to know.

Within the enormity of it, a wave of water splashed ever so close to her feet. It tussled her from the awe of the moment as she heard the familiar voice of God say, "Watch me."

"I double dog dare ya to get my feet wet!" she laughed as if nothing mattered more than seeing God show off for her.

There it was. The playful game had begun. She intently watched the waves, trying to predict which one would cross her feet and giggled when one came close.

"Almost!" She played back.

The biggest and most furious hardly reached the shore, and from time to time the milder ones would come just near enough to measure a couple feet or sometimes inches away. Often the water would go past her on either side, but not touch her.

"You can do better than that," she teased.

She began to clock the regularity of the close calls and found, about every twenty minutes or so, another one would almost make it. The water continued its own pattern, sometimes washing up in other places higher then where she sat and sometimes not at all. Each wave was a gleeful testament to her faith. She knew, if she waited, God would do it.

There is a funny thing about the glistening on the horizon. As time passes, it moves ever so slowly toward the west and further into the distance. She noticed the sun was no longer overhead but shifting away. Her face and shins felt sunburned as she waited with dry feet. Just about the time she began to wonder if she were a stiff-necked fool taunting God, a white beach bird - a gull, dove, or who knows - meandered in front of her chair to wait with her. Poised gracefully, it looked toward the horizon. A couple times it glanced back at her as if saying, "We can do this." Then the bird returned its gaze toward the ocean.

"*The Holy Spirit?*" she asked herself.

For nearly a half hour, the bird stood there, assuring her it was faith, not taunting. She believed God would do it, and she believed He wanted her to enjoy it, every silly little drop.

A couple hours passed. She contemplated if she should move her chair just a little closer to make it easier for God. Yet in her question, she felt foolish. "*Would God be disappointed if she did? Had she learned nothing?*" Waiting was for her, not for God. She nestled back into her concentration. There was nowhere for her to be. Nothing else mattered. It was just her and God. "*What was the hurry?*" She waited past the time any sane or even patient person would have stayed.

In continuing, her fullness of God grew. Each time a surge of water came close, she knew it wasn't time yet. Perhaps stretching her feet a couple more inches, she could have called it God, or she could be still.

At one point she knew, even if she left, it would have been fine for she believed God could have gotten her feet wet or not. It didn't really matter any longer because she was with Him. Hours clocked by, the sun moved west toward setting, and the waves stayed unpredictably consistent. Finally her mind stopped wandering, guessing, or even counting. The peace she believed was on the other side of eternity breathed heavily in her spirit. It did surpass all understanding, guarding her heart and mind from the abuse of intrusions. The void between her and life was purely, translucent white, no longer heavy but instead full, absolute, and splendid. She closed her eyes to thank God for a beautiful day with dry feet. "*Who could ask for more?*"

Without warning, prediction, or the subtlest announcement, the wave came in quietly with forces behind it carrying water over her feet. Not marginally but totally steadily washing the sand out from underneath them. Her heart leapt as she imagined the child in Elizabeth's womb had upon greeting Mary, the mother of Jesus. She wanted to explode into dance, to sing and to rejoice! Not simply because God had washed her feet but because finally she had the faith to wait for it, to experience God's presence on this side of eternity.

Placed across the toes on her left foot, a sprig from a plant lay as evidence it too had been washed. It was a sentimental gift, souvenir, and blessing from her Yahweh as tangible evidence she could take with her, symbolizing indeed God was present. Something was new about her, a creation. The old was gone, and the new was here. She had met the stranger within herself. The one who wanted to walk into the ocean had fallen to sleep the afternoon before. Today she played with God, with His rules and promises. She had what she yearned for on this earth. Discovering how to honor the fullness of God, as she waited until an invitation to join Him in eternity came from His perfect timing and not that of a sleeping stranger. While in her heart she planned her course, God had established her steps.

"You will only find yourself in the beauty of my creation," He softly whispered.